Acknowledgements:

Thank you Daniel for your presence, for your tender heart, for holding my hand as we walk the streets of this wonderful life together.

Thank you my beautiful children, Jane, Tim, Sam, Joe and Ben, for bringing so much love and joy to my life. I am so proud of you all.

Thank you Tim and Susie for your love, for witnessing my entire life, for always seeing me.

Thank you Paul for your constant encouragement and support – for the love that we share – for our children.

Thank you Michael and Jules for cosy bed space when I'm in London and for all your love and support – and Dao, Amida, Nikki and Benita for being my family in Devon, Sura-land.

Thank you Andy McCullough for sharing your own story, for helping me sense what life for a child living on the street is really like and for all your wonderful support.

A big thank you to Rob, Kate and everyone else at Railway Children, and to John, Stephen, Moira, Claire and everyone else at The Big Issue Foundation for being so wonderfully enthusiastic and helpful – and for coming up with so many great ideas.

Thank you Eve for your enduring commitment to my work, for your love, for our heart sharing.

Thank you Lizzie and Rachel for your patience, care and editorial expertise. I feel so blessed to have your support.

Thank you Eliz for the gorgeous cover design, I love it!

Thank you everyone else from HarperCollins who's involved in some way or other with my books. I have so much appreciation for all the hard work that you do.

Thank you Mike and Pete – I'm blown away and touched beyond measure by the incredible gifts you're laying at my feet.

Thank you Sophie for being the first reader of *Invisible Girl* and offering your helpful comments.

I have such gratitude for all the people I never get to meet – those who plant and cut the sustainable forests, make the paper, print the pages, wrap and pack and drive and stack and sell my books – without you *Invisible Girl* would be left drifting in my imagination – Thank you for the part that you play in bringing my books into being.

Thank you Adam for seeing me when I couldn't see myself.

Thank you to the space in which we all appear – in and as this…

Love Love Love x

Afterword by John Bird - Founder and Editor in Chief at The Big Issue

Can we stop children from running away? Can we reduce the vulnerability of the child when they are out there on their own? Places of safety near home, crash pads, and support need creating. Workers who can envisage what a child is going through need to prevent the poor home life leading to the streets. Charities like 'Railway Children' need our support and our attention. For once you get to the streets, the sharks and the piranhas are there for you to fall into the hands of.

The streets the homeless walk, I walked many decades ago. I slept down the back of cinemas and hotels, in little gardens and up alleys. There was always a threat. There was always someone to prey off boys like me, who had only just made it into their teens. But it was a rare enough thing then for a boy like me to rear up against the violence of home life and seek the streets as a better option, rather than stay in a badly behaving family.

Now, in the new century, I would dread to face street life. The threats are even greater. There are no longer the patrolling policemen who roamed in search of the rough sleeper. We now live in a more dislocated society and it is reflected in the amounts of children that reach our streets and seek solace in the most dangerous of places.

We have to tell stories and we have to read stories. We have to read books like *Invisible Girl* and be inspired to do something about children running away. We have to ensure that there is support for children who have abandoned hope and gone off to inhabit the threatening world of street life. I hope that this work will help us understand that we need to shake up a society that can produce so many runaways. That fails children who should have a safety net that works.

Once, a policeman brought a girl of sixteen to the Big Issue offices. She was desperate, having some problems with her exams and her family's expectations. She came from what by the look of her was a good home. But even that did not stop her from feeling that she could not face home life and school life any more, or from choosing a desperate act.

The suffering of children needs not to lead to street life. But if it does, we need the supporting net to pick them up and carry them to places of safety. Away from the ever watchful eyes of those who would exploit them. Many *Big Issue* vendors began their journey to the streets by running away as a youngster. We want to play our part in helping young people think differently about what it can mean to become homeless; our schools education packs aim to do just that.

The streets are worse than anything I encountered in my childhood. And for that reason alone I want to support books like *Invisible Girl*. And support the work of people who try to provide an answer to children's vulnerability. Please encourage others to read this book generously. Tell everyone, spread the word.

Visit www.bigissue.org.uk and www.bigissue.com

The Big Issue is a registered charity by the Charity Commission in England & Wales (no. 1049077).

Charity No. 1049077

Turn over for more great reads by

Kate Maryon x

Maya wishes she could go surfing and hang out on the beach, but as an only child her parents are pretty overprotective.
Cat has the freedom to do what she likes – her mum barely looks after herself...

But now Maya's family are adopting Cat and suddenly their lives collide. As tensions rise and secrets surface, can Maya and Cat ever be friends, let alone sisters?

*"We talk about everything. Dad and me. About all
the mysteries inside of us. About all our wonderings
of the world. But tomorrow my dad goes to war.
Then what will I do?"*

Jemima's dad is in the Army and he's off to
Afghanistan for six whole months. Her mum's about
to have another baby and Gran's head is filled with
her own wartime memories. So while Mima is
sending Dad millions of guardian angels to keep
him safe, who is looking out for her?

A Million Angels
Kate Maryon x

"It was just school to me. I'd been there since I was seven years old. But I'm not there any more, I'm here and I need to get on and get used to it, just like all the other changes in my life."

Liberty is sure there's more to life than getting good exam results and earning lots of money, but her super-rich, workaholic dad doesn't agree. And when Dad's business goes bust and there's no money left, Liberty's whole world is turned upside down...

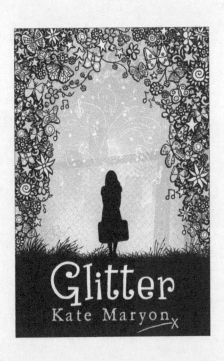

Glitter
Kate Maryon

*"The page is staring at me waiting for words, but I don't
even know where to start. I'd quite like
to begin the letter with something like,
Dear Mum, Thanks for ruining my life,
but I don't think that's the kind of letter that
Auntie Cass has in mind."*

Tiff's sparkling world comes crashing down when
her mum commits a crime. Packed off to live with
family in the dullest place on the planet – and without
Mum around – everything seems to
lose its shine . . .

Invisible Girl

Kate Maryon is officially addicted to writing. She also loves meeting her readers when she goes into schools to give talks and run writing workshops and is always so touched by the many emails and letters she receives from them telling her how much they enjoy her books.

Kate lives in Somerset with her husband, Daniel, and their cheeky kittens, Misha and Loki. Sadly, her gorgeous dog, Ellie, died last year ☹ She loves spending time with her grown-up children and all her gorgeous friends and feels so happy and blessed to be living the life she lives.

But wherever she is, whatever she's doing, there's always a story running through her imagination, the shadow of a character forming in her heart.

Kate loves chocolate, films, eating out, reading, writing, and lying on sunny beaches. She still dislikes peppermint and honey.

Also by Kate Maryon

Shine

Glitter

A Million Angels

A Sea of Stars

Invisible Girl

Kate Maryon

HarperCollins *Children's Books*

First published in Great Britain by HarperCollins *Children's Books* in 2013
HarperCollins *Children's Books* is a division of HarperCollins*Publishers* Ltd,
77–85 Fulham Palace Road, Hammersmith, London, W6 8JB.

The HarperCollins website address is: www.harpercollins.co.uk

6

Invisible Girl

ISBN 978-0-00-746690-0

Kate Maryon asserts the moral right to be identified as the author of this work.

Printed and bound in England by
Clays Ltd, St Ives plc

MIX
Paper from
responsible sources
FSC C007454

FSC™ is a non-profit international organisation established to promote
the responsible management of the world's forests. Products carrying the
FSC label are independently certified to assure consumers that they come
from forests that are managed to meet the social, economic and
ecological needs of present and future generations,
and other controlled sources.

Find out more about HarperCollins and the environment at
www.harpercollins.co.uk/green

For Dawne, Susie, Susannah, Rachel, Helen,
Emma, Becky and Clea…
May we dance in this glorious fire of tea-drinking,
wine-sipping, heart-sharing friendship until our old bones return
to dust and all that laughter and all those tears are heard as Love,
echoing through the glittering hallways of eternity. X

For Mathilda, Freddie and Ella…
For your truly wonderful dads, Mike and Pete, you touch my heart
with your enthusiasm and generosity – thank you both so much. x

Foreword by Andy McCullough – Head of Policy for the charity Railway Children

You may be surprised to know 100,000 children in the UK run away from home or care every year. Many are thrown out, no longer wanted in the family. The majority of children say family problems and issues are the main reason for them running.

Often when you end up running away you feel you have got rid of your problems; however, you usually substitute them for other problems. Being out on the streets is lonely, cold and really dangerous. We know that there are always people who will exploit young people and use them for profit and power.

I have worked in the field of social care for over twenty-seven years, but some of my training was as a child myself, spending a lot of time on the streets, having run away. I met a lot of good people whilst out there, people who had grown up in care, been kicked out by their family or had become detached, but always, like a dark shadow, there were people who wanted to use you to make sure they were better off.

Gabriella's story is an important one to hear. Who knows, it may make you think a little differently when you pass a child on the streets...

Railway Children is a registered charity, no.1058991
Visit www.railwaychildren.org.uk

Fighting for street children

Foreword by Andy McCullough – Head of Policy for the charity Railway Children

You may be surprised to know 100,000 children in the UK run away from home or care every year. Many are thrown out, no longer wanted in the family. The majority of children are family problems and issues are the main reason for them running.

Often when rounded up running away, you feel you have nowhere of your own place; however, we hereby substitute them to other problems. Keep out on the streets is for... to cold and costly threesome. We know that there are always people who will... place young people and that they either profit or power.

I have worked in the field of social care for over twenty-seven years... for some of my training was as a child myself, spending a lot of time on the streets, having run away. I met a lot of good people while out there, people who had grown up in care, not looked out of their family, or had become destitute, but always like a rack ahead... there were people who wanted to do youth to make sure they were better off.

Children's story is an important one to hear. Who knows, it may make you think a little differently when you pass a child on the streets.

Railway Children is a registered charity no. 1058991
Visit www.railwaychildren.org.uk

RAILWAY
ch*ldren
fighting for street children

Then

**Most days drift by like clouds. Others burn
deep into your life and make a blister, like a
bright white moon in a black night sky.
And you're left wondering, forever.**

Then, I might as well have been invisible for all Dad and
Amy cared. They'd been busy making massive decisions
about my life without even thinking about me, or
bothering about how I might feel. They'd obviously
been plotting and planning for weeks, whispering
under the covers at night, painting the walls of our flat
with lies.

The day had been creeping towards me like a tiger

in the dark with its amber eyes glinting, for ages. The shouting had been getting worse. Dad had started spending more and more money we didn't have. He'd broken his promise and started using credit cards again, to keep Amy happy. But it didn't work. Amy just got madder and madder, her screeching making her face flush pink and her lips turn white with rage.

What's strange is that the day it actually happened everything seemed so normal. Dad ignored me, his eyes glued to *Daybreak* on the telly and Amy hogged the bathroom for so long I thought I was going to wet myself. In the end I couldn't wait any longer, so I picked up my bag and raced off to school with a piece of toast and jam between my teeth without even saying goodbye.

If I'd known I was never going to sleep in my bed again or sit on our sofa or lie in our bath under the bubbles, I might've snuggled down in the warm a bit longer, soaked up that feeling of home. I might have given Dad a kiss, begged him to change his mind; at least I could've asked him why. I'd definitely have grabbed more toast.

Toast would've been good because I had no idea how hungry I'd get, or how cold.

The most annoying thing though, apart from what Dad did, is that he didn't put my little photo of Beckett with the letter. I hadn't seen or heard from Beckett or Mum for seven years, nothing at all since the day they left. So not having the photo made everything so much harder.

Chapter 1

When Amy arrived

Things were fine when it was just Dad and me. We never really talked about anything important, but we were OK. I missed Beckett loads and wished he could've stayed with us, but I was relieved Mum had gone. I hadn't felt scared in the morning for ages. I hadn't had to hide under my covers at night, smothering my sobs by biting on Blue Bunny's ear. And although Dad never bought flowers, like my best friend Grace's mum does every Friday, our flat was still nice; it was our cosy home.

But that was before Amy came along and ruined everything. I could tell she didn't want me around from the start. The way she kept glaring at me and sighing; the way she got into a huff if Dad so much as even looked at me. She kept clinging to him like tangled ivy up a wall, batting her spidery eyelashes, whispering in his ear. If I were a piece of old furniture, Amy could have taken me along to the tip with all the other old stuff that belonged to Mum. It would've made it much easier for her to chuck me out of her life, to pretend I'd never existed.

The worst thing was, Dad didn't even tell me she was moving in. I was there, digging through the iceberg in the freezer, looking for chips to go with eggs for our tea and she arrived with a million black bin liners, bulging with stuff…

"Where on earth d'you expect me to put my things, Dave," she says, clattering up the hallway, "when this place is so full of junk?"

She opens and closes our cupboard doors, slams around the flat like she owns it. She goes into my room and starts rearranging my stuff, kicking my scrapbook things under my bed, picking bits of fluff off the floor.

I can't believe my eyes. She stands there with her hands on her hips, tutting like a bird, rolling her eyes like a mad person.

"Put them wherever you like, babe," Dad says. "You know, make yourself at home."

I wanted to punch Dad then, to wake him up. He'd gone all floppy and pathetic like he used to be with Mum, like a big stupid fat lump of dough. Why did he do this? Why can't he tell her to get lost so we can eat our eggs and chips in peace and watch the telly?

Dad opens his arms wide and pulls Amy in so tight his big belly bulges like whale blubber around her.

"And you, Mister," she says, pulling away from him and jabbing at his belly with her sharp red fingernail, "need to shed a few pounds." She pats him like he was her puppy. "Can't have my man being a big old fathead, can I?"

"Look, babe," says Dad, slapping Amy's bum, "what's mine is yours. You're the woman of the house now. Do what you like with the place. I don't care."

That was the wrong thing to say because:

1. I do care.

2. Amy does just that.

Later on she starts pulling the flat apart, rearranging it, putting all her stinky air freshener plug-in things and stupid ornaments all over the place. She clutters up the bathroom with loads of body scrubs and sprays and mountains of make-up.

"Ew!" she says, leaning over the chip pan, almost choking me to death in a swirl of perfume. "What on earth d'you call that?"

My cheeks burn hotter than the chip fat.

"Egg and chips," I say. "I'm making tea for Dad."

Amy laughs like a hyena in *The Lion King*. She rests her hand on her forehead, dramatically, and starts staggering about the kitchen on her pink high heels.

"You're not seriously gonna eat that rubbish she's making you, Dave, are you? You might die from food poisoning! Quick! Quick! Fumigate the place! We might all die!"

Dad leans against the fridge and sighs.

I freeze, stiller than a statue, and watch the edges of the chips frizzle and burn while these huge invisible hands slide inside me and scrunch my tummy up tight.

"Nah, babe," Dad says. "You're right! We've got a real woman in the house now; we don't need to eat that old muck. You can cook proper grub for us, right, babe?"

Amy laughs and rolls her eyes, the little red veins threading over them like rivers.

"If you think I'm gonna be a slave to your kitchen, Dave," she says, poking his belly, "you've got another think coming. I'm your girlfriend, remember, not your freaking wife!"

Dad opens the fridge and peers inside. He sniffs a carton of gone-off milk, reeling backwards with the stink.

"How about a takeaway?" says Amy. "You know... celebration time!"

She starts digging in his pockets for his wallet, tugging at his shirt, her bony hands moving all over him. Dad pulls away; his ears glowing as red as a throbbing sore.

"Not tonight, eh, babe?" he says, nudging her away. "Let's save it for the weekend. We'll have the egg and chips, shall we? Gabriella's done them now. I promised her we'd sit together to eat and watch telly. Shame to waste them."

Amy puckers her lips so tight they remind me of a hamster's bottom.

"You're not gonna turn into a mean man now I've moved in, are you, Dave?" she says, jabbing her elbow in his ribs. "You know what they say about mean men."

A line of sweat bubbles above Dad's top lip. He pulls his wallet out of his pocket and digs his fat fingers in to get at the cash. He sighs and all his strength kind of drains away like water.

"All right then," he says, "anything you like." He turns to me. "Gabriella, run down to Chang's, will you?"

"Good idea, Dave," says Amy, giggling, wriggling her way into his arms, nibbling at his ear. She glares at me and holds Dad tight like she's won him as a prize.

I ignore Dad and watch the burny bits creep along the chips until every one is black and smoke is billowing into the kitchen. Amy starts flapping her arms like mad.

"I'm gonna choke, Dave!" she squawks. "Open the window, will you, you stupid old fat bum!" She puts her hands on her hips and stares at me. "I'm the woman of the house, Gabriella Midwinter, your dad just said so.

So you'll keep your grubby hands out of my kitchen and get sharpish at tidying up that bedroom of yours. Do you hear?"

My heart thumps in my ears. I glare at her through the swirls of black smoke. My room is none of her business.

"I like it in a mess," I say. "I know where everything is and Dad doesn't mind."

She moves towards me, her shoes clip-clopping on the kitchen floor, her waggling finger pointing. "Well, young lady," she says, pushing her face so close to mine I can see the streaks of fake tan on her cheeks, "things are about to change round here. I'm the boss now. So you'd better get used to it."

My legs are trembling. "But it's not your flat, Amy," I say. "It's ours. And Dad's the boss. I like my room how it is."

"This place is a disgrace," she snaps. "The council would slap a health warning on it if they came for a visit!"

I wish Dad would charge forward and pull her away from me. I wish he'd tell her I can have my room how I like. Instead, he pulls a can of lager out the fridge, snaps it open and takes a long cool sip. He pours a glass of wine for Amy that reminds me of blood, and looks at her and then at me. He sighs, handing me a wodge of cash. I glare at him.

"Dad!" I say. "We can't afford takeaway—"

"Gabriella," he interrupts, "don't be boring. Be a good girl and go and get the food."

"And make sure you get my order right, Miss Flappy Ears," says Amy. "I want beef with black bean sauce."

I'm glad to leave the flat. The air outside is warm and the sun's turning red in the sky. I stare at it for ages, watching it sink lower and lower. I wish I had some paints with me. I wish I were a proper artist with a real easel and proper brushes and a little stool and an actual canvas. I would really love to paint that sun.

The queue at Chang's is long. But I don't mind. I sit and watch the fishes swim round and round the tank, in and out of a little blue castle that's nestled in the gravel. Round and round and round, weaving through the plants. I wonder if they ever get bored?

I feel like a fish sometimes, going from home to

school and back again. Round and round, to town or the park or Grace's. Dad and me never go anywhere fun. We never do anything special. If Grace invites me on one of her famous expeditions my tank gets a little bit bigger for the day, but it doesn't happen very often. Zoe and Elsie from my class have amazing lives full of glitter and lip-gloss shimmer, full of popcorn and pony trekking and soft pink leotards with white net tutus for ballet dancing.

I like Friday afternoons when the Play Rangers come to our estate and make us hot chocolate and we toast marshmallows on a fire. We build camps from blue plastic and rotten wood, and run around playing games, squealing at the top of our lungs. But I can still see our flat from the green. I can still see Mrs McKlusky's tartan slippers fringed with the soft tufts of cotton, shuffling about. I can still hear her mumbling words rude enough to make your ears sting.

Grace came to Play Rangers once and thought it was the best thing ever. My tummy felt warm then, that I had something special to share. Dad keeps promising he'll come and watch us one day. He keeps promising to fix us a rope swing in the tree on the green.

I order crispy duck for Amy and wish I could tell Chang to put poison on it. But I don't in case Dad eats it or me. I worry in case one of us dies or if Amy dies and Dad gets sent to prison. Sometimes my heart burns hot with worry. My tummy gets in tangles because who would care for me if Dad was gone? Grace is lucky. Grace has a nice mum *and* a nice dad. She has two grannies *and* a grandpa and all sorts of special aunties and uncles and cousins who send her things in the post. Things wrapped in shiny paper with ribbons so colourful I just want to snip them up and make beautiful patterns with the scraps.

When I get back home the flat is quiet with a note on Dad's bedroom door saying, DO NOT DISTURB. I push my ear against the cold paintwork to listen. Dad's laughing, Amy's squealing, their music is blaring.

I grab a fork from the kitchen, shut myself in the front room and put the telly on so loud I know that Mrs McKlusky will bang on the wall with her broom.

I don't care about Dad and Amy. I'm glad they're not with me because I can stretch right out on the sofa with my feet up and all the cushions are mine. I can watch my favourite hospital programme in peace. There's been this big car crash and people are dead, but some are still alive, groaning. My favourite paramedic girl with the soft, kind voice is coming to the rescue. I watch carefully, trying to work out how the make-up artists make all the gashes and bruises look so real.

When I've finished my chicken chow mein I lick my fingers and slide my tongue across my lips to keep the taste going on for a little bit longer. I dig into the mountain of prawn crackers, dipping them in the sweet chilli sauce, cramming them into my mouth, tasting them prickle and melt. Dad's sweet and sour pork smells so good I can't stop myself from dipping my fingers in its sticky red juice and licking them like lollipops.

And I know he won't mind because you could easily lay my dad on the floor and wipe your muddy feet all over him and he wouldn't say one thing. You could slap him round the face, like Mum used to, and he'd just slide off into the bedroom to hide. Like I'd slide under my bed and get as close to the wall as I could. As far away as possible, so she couldn't get to me with her sharp slaps or see how much the big purple bruises they left on my skin hurt.

I can't stop fretting that Dad'll miss his tea and be starving. Amy's food is sitting on the edge of the coffee table, staring at me, daring me to touch it. I won't eat it. I'd never do that. But this idea starts swimming round and round my head like Chang's fishes, pressing in on my skin.

I write 'beef in black bean sauce' on the lid so it looks like Chang made a mistake with the order. Then I peel off the lid and rest it on the side. I breathe in crispy duck dare. I put my face close and let spit dribble out and melt into the sauce. I stir my fork round and round then put the lid back on so neat that unless Amy is a detective she'll never find out.

When my favourite lady on the hospital programme has finished crying into her boyfriend's arms because she didn't save the people in time, I watch this other one about cooking in Italy. They make this yummy red sauce and powdery cheese pasta with green basil sprigged on top. They show you the sights and it's so real I feel like I'm actually in the car with the man with the rusty beard. I'm driving down the avenues of tall trees, past golden fields. I'm drinking the cappuccino hot milk froth with chocolate. Like it's *me*, far away from here.

And when we get to the art gallery, in Florence, I hold my breath because the paintings are amazing. There's one that's so huge it's impossible to work out how you might even paint it. It has this woman standing in a big shell and all these other people swooping and swooshing around her.

The marble sculpture of someone called *David* is the best. Grace would've laughed her socks off if she were watching because David's naked. Imagine having a huge chunk of cool white marble in front of you, all the chisels and hammers you need. Imagine chipping away until you're covered in white dust and your hands are sore and the person inside steps out and stops waiting forever for someone to find them.

Later in bed, my duvet is tangled and I'm hot, sticky and sweaty with sleep, when I hear Amy in the kitchen. I hear the microwave ping. I hear her fork clink, clinking on the plate.

"Chang's rubbish at getting his orders right, but this crispy duck is gorgeous, Dave," she says. "Totally gorgeous!"

I snuggle into Blue Bunny and stroke the soft silky label on his ear, the bit where Beckett wrote his name in red biro before he left.

Chapter 2

I hate my room. It's so tidy because of Amy. She does this inspection thing every day, checking round the flat, making sure no germs are lurking like swamp monsters in the shadows. I wish they were. I wish armies of them would creep out of their hiding place and eat her. I wish they'd pull her down to their dark red cauldrons and mix her up to make poison. There are so many words on my lips for Amy. Bad words that would scorch your ears and make the lady in the sweet shop shoo the big boys out. But I'm not stupid enough to say them, so my tummy makes a big fist around them and holds them safe inside. When Amy's done her inspection I close my bedroom door and mess things up again.

She's mean to my dad too. I feel sorry for him. Last week while I was on the green drinking creamy hot chocolate with Grace and the Play Rangers I caught him staring out of the window with this pale face, looking so lost and sad.

After, I made him a coffee and we sat quietly together listening to the football results on the telly. And I loved him smiling when Arsenal won. I loved that we did a high five and I felt the warmth of his hand for the first time in ages. But then Amy came in and threw us off the sofa so she could plump up the cushions and put them neatly in pairs.

Before Amy, we only ever vacuumed the floor on special occasions. Now she makes Dad push the vacuum cleaner around every day and do all these stupid exercises at the same time. He looks stupid in the pink rubber gloves and plastic muscleman pinafore she got him for when he does the washing-up.

"Dave!" she says, inspecting the sink. "You haven't even bleached it yet, have you? We'll all get salmonella at this rate."

And then she sprays the whole world with Spring Breeze air freshener that stings our eyes and chokes our throats.

When Amy's out at Zumba class I get the chance to sit close to Dad and watch the telly and feel like it's just him and me again. And I want to tell him everything. I want to say it all out loud, all the words twisting through me, getting tangled up inside. But I don't know where to start. I'm too scared of making him cross or upsetting him.

"Do you like Amy, Dad?" I whisper. "Like, really like her?"

Dad sighs and stares at *Top Gear*. He snaps open his next can of lager and I watch the foamy bubbles fizz up through the opening and dribble down the sides.

"I mean, we don't really *need* her," I say. "Do we? I think we were much better without her. And I'm worried about money. The landlord said if you miss the rent again he'll evict us, remember, Dad?"

Dad flicks the TV from channel to channel. He sips and sips and sips.

"Don't you start on at me as well," he says, without

looking at me. "It might be hard for you to understand, but I don't just *like* Amy, Gabriella, I *love* her. I'm a man possessed by a beautiful woman. I'm sorry if you don't like it, but I can't help myself."

His words fly at me like a football in the park, punching me with a cold hard thud in the tummy. I think I might be sick. He's never said he loves *me*. He's never said anything *that* nice about me, *ever*. I rub my face. I bend over to re-tie my laces.

Dad pats his wobbly tummy and peers at me from under his fringe. He sip, sip, sips his lager. "I reckon…" he says.

Then he stops talking. The air between us pulls tight and makes me hold my breath. Suddenly it feels just like the day he said Mum and Beckett were leaving.

"I reckon," he says, "if I can shed a few pounds, Amy might even marry me. What d'you think of that, eh? And I promise you Amy'll let you be a bridesmaid if you keep your room tidy and start doing the stuff she asks. The pair of you could dress up all posh and lovely. Don't worry about the rent, Gabriella. I've got it all under control. You just have to learn to trust your old dad."

He rummages in his pocket then pulls out a small square box and opens it up. "And when she sees this little baby," he chuckles, holding a diamond ring between his fat finger and thumb so it glitters in the light, "she might not even care about my tummy!"

I fly into my room, slam the door and bite back the sour tears that are rising in my throat. I can't let myself think about what Dad's just said, so I pull out my box of art scraps and scatter them across the floor.

I cut and rip shiny sweet wrappers and bits of paper, making them into tiny bricks. I draw the outline of a house on a fresh clean page and glue the shiny bricks on one by one. I make little red roof tiles out of material I found at a car boot sale and a trail of grey smoke coming from the chimney out of a pair of Dad's old pants. I colour in a bright blue front door and put loads of sunflowers in the garden like in the Italy programme. I cut a girl's face from a magazine and stick her on the picture so she's looking out of the window at the flowers.

I pick up my little photo of Beckett that lives on my bedside table with the special book I won in the school art competition about famous artists. I stare at his face and wish he would leap out and talk to me.

"I wish you were here, Beckett," I whisper. "Where are you?"

In the photo he was twelve, same as I am now, which means he'll be nineteen now. Nineteen is so old! I flick through my magazine and I find a picture of a man with brown hair just like Beckett's. I cut him out, glue him in the garden and bend his arm so he's waving up at me. Then I hear the door slam and Amy's voice screeching like a parrot in a cage.

"Are you ready, Dave, or what?"

I hear Dad shuffling into the hallway.

"What?" he says. "Ready for what?"

"That's typical," she spits. "You men are all the same. Total let-downs!"

"Babe," he says. "Come 'ere, darling. Wassup?"

"Wassup?" she screeches. "I'll tell you 'wassup', Dave. You *promised* to take me out. You *promised* me a romantic night, you stupid fat bum. Just the two of us, without Miss Untidy Ungrateful Flappy Ears butting in, remember?"

I put my headphones on and fill my brain with tunes. I make some lovely grass with scraps of green thread on my picture and some soft white clouds from cotton wool. I stick more white pages around my picture and start filling them up too. I add a swimming pool and an outdoor cinema. I build a treehouse out of matches and make a swing from bits of string. I add a village with pavements and little stone cottages in a row. I add a dog, a shop, a hairdressers, a chippy and a Chang's. I cut out cars and a lady on a bicycle and loads of smiley people walking down the road.

When the front door slams it's so loud the floor shudders under me. I pull my headphones out and listen. I peep into the hall.

I don't even care if they've gone. It's better here without them.

I make myself cheese on toast, leaving the butter and the knife and the crumbs all over the worktop and I stretch out on the sofa with my shoes on, snuggling in front of the telly.

It's mostly boring stuff until this murder thing comes on. It's exciting at first, but then knives start flashing and the man's big black boots send shivers down my spine. I wish Dad were here with me, and then I could watch it, no problem.

When it gets really gory and this woman's voice is screaming I cover my face with my hands. I wish I could switch it off, but I can't move. I can't switch to another channel because I have to make sure that they catch the murderer in case he's actually real, in case he's actually lurking about outside our flats.

It's not until I feel chilly that I look up at the clock and notice it's half-past twelve. The murderer man is stalking around in this underground car park, hiding in the shadows. A lady is heading towards her car, but she can't see him. I scream at her to hurry up, to run away, to lock herself in her car and call the police. She's walking so slowly, her high-heeled shoes clip-clopping, scraping on the concrete.

"Run!" I shriek. "Run, you stupid lady, run!"

Something creaks in the hall. I freeze. My heart pounds in my ears and ripples through my skin. The murderer man's eyes glint in the moonlight.

"Dad!" I call out. "Is that you?"

The murderer music starts howling and the lady is all shrieking voice and clip-clop running, panting, out of breath. But the murderer man is faster. His boots are slapping the ground in long strides, quickly catching her up.

"Dad!"

I flick the telly off and my ears thump as I drown in the silence.

"Dad!" I whisper. "Dad, where are you?"

I grab Blue Bunny, hold him close and stroke the silky label on his ear. Beckett gave him to me the day I was born and even though he's a bit battered he's still the best thing in the world. I wish Beckett were here now. He would know what to do.

I stay frozen in the chair for hours, watching the clock tick, tick, tick on the wall. Someone is stalking round the flat, I'm sure of it. They're creaking the floorboards, shuffling into my room, humming a scary tune. I pick up one of Amy's heavy ornaments and creep around the flat, shuffling silently behind the noise, following it from room to room. When I'm in the bathroom I hear it clinking in the kitchen. When I'm in the kitchen I hear it thudding in the hall. I walk round and round for ages, too scared to find it, too scared that I won't. Then I think about Mum. What if it's her? What if she's come back and she's hiding in the shadows, waiting for me?

My heart's pounding so loud in my ears I run to my room and hide. It's the only safe place left.

When I wake up the morning sun is streaming through the window, filling my room with a soft, pinky light. And for a while I can't work out why I'm on the floor, tucked right underneath my bed, as close to the wall as I can get. Then the murderer's face looms in my brain and Mum's mean smile flashes shark teeth in my eyes.

"Dad!" I shout.

I know it's stupid, because our flat's really small and he would have heard me shouting if he were home, but I can't help racing from room to room to check.

"Dad! Dad! Where are you?"

My heart starts thudding. I lie down on his bed, rest my face on his pillow and breathe in the greasy stink his hair has left behind. It's not a nice smell, not anything you'd want to put in a bottle and sell, but it is my dad. Then I remember all the empty lager cans on the front room floor. I leap up and count them. I peer out of the window searching for his car, and then the hospital programme sneers in my eyes. What if he's had a car crash and died? Seven cans of lager are too much to drink when you're driving. What if he's really hurt and lying in hospital somewhere? Or what if he's run someone over and they're dead and Dad's at the police station? How will I know? If he goes to prison, then what about me?

I try calling, but his phone's switched off. I try Amy's and it's the same. I switch on *Daybreak* to fill the flat with the sound of laughter. I huddle on Dad's chair with my knees hunched up to my chest, biting a scab on my arm until it bleeds. *Please come home, Dad, please! I'll be really good forever. I'll do all the washing-up for you. I won't even complain about Amy any more, I'll do everything she says, just please come home!*

I open the front door and pace up and down the balcony that connects all the flats in our block together.

I peer over the edge, stretching my eyes across the green where the Play Rangers go, past the cars, as far as I can see.

I go back indoors. I put the kettle on and make a cup of tea with two sugars and watch it turn cold. I pour a bowl of cereal and stir it round and round until the milk has melted it to mush. I put my uniform on and pack my school bag in a daze. Should I go to school? Should I stay home? Should I call 999 for help?

Fear is nesting inside me, curled up tight in the fist-sized pit where my ribs meet at the front. It's sitting there with its jaggedy hair and its bright eyes, watching. I lie on Dad's bed again and count to a thousand. I whisper to Blue Bunny that it's all going to be OK. I go outside again and peer over the balcony.

And that's when I can't believe my eyes!

They're there.

Standing in the middle of the green! Kissing!

"Dad!" I call. Tears, that I blink away, gather and twist like a hard knot of wood in my throat.

"What happened, Dad? Where were you all night?"

Amy stares up at me. "What are you then, Gabriella,"

she snaps, "his keeper or what?"

She clatters up the stairwell; Dad puffing up behind her with his head drooped low.

"If you hadn't noticed," Amy says, "we're grown-ups and grown-ups don't have to ask to go out. Let alone from a twelve-year-old with manners like scum! And I hope you haven't messed the place up, Gabriella. I hope your bed is made. It might be nice if just occasionally you appreciated me for bringing a bit of order to your life instead of nagging on about where we've been."

Mrs McKlusky opens her front door and scuttles outside. "What's the racket?" she says, twitching her eyes. "It's not even eight o'clock. Some of us like to drink our morning cup of tea in peace! It's not too much to ask, is it?"

Amy turns on her. "And you can shut it!" she sneers. "D'you hear me? Keep your sharp beak out of other people's business, you nosy old bat!"

Dad sighs and bundles us indoors. "Calm down, Gabriella," he says. "What's all the fuss? Nobody's died, have they?"

I glare at him.

I fold my arms across my chest and turn my back on him, anger rising like a flooding river inside me. Although I'm angry with Dad I wish he'd hold me tight like that day Mum and Beckett left. I wish he would say something nice to me. "You stayed out all night, Dad!" I shout. "Where were you?"

Dad presses his hand over his mouth, stopping his words from tumbling out.

"Where were you, Dad?" I whisper, tears escaping from my eyes. "I thought you'd had a car crash! I thought you'd died! It's all *her* fault – you never did anything like this before Amy was around!"

I dig my nails into my palms and wish they were Amy's flesh. Dad doesn't say one word, he won't even look at me. He just flops on the sofa and sighs. He snaps open another can of lager.

"Oh, give it a rest, Miss Doom and Gloom. We're getting *married*," Amy says in a sharp voice, flopping next to Dad and sliding into his arms. "There, I've said it. Your dad is no longer your property, he's mine. It's official and it's going to happen whether you like it or not and for your *information* it's not up to Dave who my bridesmaids are, it's up to me. And I'm having my best mates. We're having an *adults only* big flash bash on a sunny beach somewhere exotic, aren't we, Dave? Somewhere far away from this old dump. It's none of your business where we were last night, Miss Flappy Ears, but if you must know, we were in a *very* expensive, *very* posh hotel! Celebrating!"

Chapter 3

When that happened

Dad's been weird since asking Amy to marry him. He's gone quieter than ever, drifting round the flat like a wisp-thin ghost. Amy's got louder and bossier, like one of those Salvador Dali paintings from my book, all twisted and unpredictable. She's spending our money on things for the wedding every single day. She's bought two dresses already so she can choose. But we're not allowed to see. She shuts herself in Dad's room with her friends and they coo over them like they were kittens. She's bought special silky underwear and these pearly shoes that shimmer. She got Dad this smart grey suit with a pink silk shirt and a purple cravat and he says he feels like a turkey all trussed up for Christmas. I'm more invisible than ever. No one's speaking to me. They wouldn't even notice if I never came home.

Amy's the only important one round here. She's high up, towering above us like a queen, making up all the rules. And I'm getting so used to being invisible that I'm shocked when Mrs Evans tells me I got an A+ for my still-life art project. She says my painting stands out from the crowd and it's going on the special display board for Parents' Evening for everyone to see. Dad won't see it, because he never bothers with Parents' Evening, but I run home quick to whisper my news to Blue Bunny.

"Here," says Amy, shoving an envelope in my hand when I get to the top of the stairs. She's standing by our front door with her sunglasses propped up on her head. "Take it, quick. I've got to go."

She squints from the sunlight and pulls her mirrored sunglasses down so I can't see her eyes.

"And take this," she says, dropping a bulging

backpack on the ground in front of me. "We put as much of your stuff in as we could."

"Amy," I say. "What are you on about?"

"It's all in the envelope," she says. "Your dad's written everything down. Come on, quick, give me your key to the flat."

I stare at the white envelope, my name scrawled across the front in Dad's loopy handwriting. I stare at the fat backpack on the ground.

"Why do you need my key?" I say. "I need it to get in. Come on, Amy, I'm desperate for a wee." Then it dawns on me.

"Oh, no! Did someone break in again?" I ask. "Did Dad have to change the locks?"

"No, dummy," says Amy, waggling her hand in front of my face. "Look, Gabriella, I did you a favour waiting for you; you should be grateful. I was worried someone might nick your stuff and then you'd be stranded. Anyway, we need to give your key back to the landlord. Your stupid dad forgot to pay the rent. Stupid fat bum he is!"

My tummy sinks to the ground and a red rage blazes inside me.

"I knew this would happen," I screech. "It's all your fault. Dad's not stupid, he's just kind. Mum used to trample all over him just like you do and it's not fair. We were OK before you came along. I told him we mustn't spend all the money. It's gone on that stupid wedding stuff you got!"

She tuts and checks her watch.

"Gabriella," she says, "I've had enough of listening to you gabble on about stuff. It's not important. You're not important. I tried to be a good mother to you and make your life better, but what thanks do I get, eh? Anyway, you're not my problem any more."

I fumble in my bag for the key, my hands fluttering like leaves.

"What are we going to do?" I say. "Where are we going to live?"

"Just be a good girl for once in your tiny life, stop asking questions and give me the key," she sneers. "Everything's explained in the letter. But think about it, Gabriella, your dad's not that kind, is he? He's known about the eviction for a few weeks now. If he was that much of a kind guy he'd have told you all about it. If he was *that* nice he'd have been waiting here to give you your bag. He'd have put you on the train and kissed you goodbye *himself*."

Her words hit me like a car, spinning me through the air, rocking me sideways. "Wh… what…" I stammer. "What train?"

"I told you," she says. "I haven't got time to stand here and explain it all. You're going on a train to your mum's and we're catching a plane to somewhere exotic. Yay!"

She waggles her fingers in my face again, her big fat diamond engagement ring glinting in the sun.

"I'm the lucky one!" she sings. "I always have been and always will be, you'll see!" Then she turns and runs down the stairs, her sandals clicking and clacking on the concrete.

"And," she shouts up at me, "don't get yourself into trouble, Gabriella, OK?"

I lean over the edge of the balcony. "Amy!" I shout. "Where's Dad? I don't understand! You can't just leave me!"

Then a smart car with a taxi sign on top screeches to

45

a halt outside our flat. Dad's in the back, his face turned away from me. Amy jumps in next to him. Everything's going in slow motion like it sometimes does in films.

"Dad!" I shout, racing down the stairs, my tummy dangling off strings, twisting and turning in knots. "Dad, what's going on?"

He doesn't even look at me; the taxi driver flashes the indicator light and zooms away. I run after them, calling "Dad" over and over, but I can't catch up and the car disappears round the corner and gets lost in the stream of traffic.

Back up the stairs I pull my phone out of my bag and call him. It goes straight through to answer phone without ringing and so does Amy's. I know they won't answer, I know they've gone, but I can't stop pressing the green button over and over and over, my shaky thumbs slipping and sliding on the keys.

"What's all the racket this time?" says Mrs McKlusky, shuffling along the balcony in her tartan slippers. She stops dead in her tracks and pins me down with her eagle eyes. "What you doing here anyway? Your dad said you was moving. I saw him heaving all your stuff out this morning. He made a right old mess of everything and then upped and left. Nonsense, it is, leaving us to clean up after him." She clacks her teeth on her tongue. "Utter nonsense."

My heart flaps inside me, a caged owl with frantic wings.

"I errrrm," I say, stuffing my phone in my pocket. "I errrrm, I forgot we'd moved, that's all, Mrs McKlusky. I'm off to meet my dad and Amy now. At our new place. Bye!"

I pick up the backpack and my school bag and quickly scoot back down the stairs. When I get out on to the road I keep my eyes on the ground. I don't want to see anyone; I don't want anyone to see me. I don't want to talk. I just keep walking and walking, clutching the chalk-white envelope in my hand.

And when I'm far away from our flats, far, far away from Mrs McKlusky's beady spy eyes, I find a bench and sit down. My hands are shaking. My shoulders are aching from the really heavy bags. I stare at the envelope. I stare at Dad's handwriting scrawled in huge letters across the front. *Gabriella.*

I trace my finger over the blue biro shapes. He didn't put a kiss. He didn't even underline it. I pull out my phone and press the green button again and again and again. I listen over and over to his voice. *"Hi, Dave here, I'm off on me hols, so don't leave a message as I won't be getting back to you anytime soon… Hi, Dave here, I'm off on me hols, so don't leave a message as I won't be getting back to you anytime soon."*

I slip my finger in the envelope and open it a tiny bit. But then panic freezes me; my heart bangs loudly and I stare at Dad's handwriting for ages. What did Amy mean about going to Mum's? We don't even know where she lives, we haven't heard from her for years. I don't even want to see her. I don't want to read the stupid letter. And I'm not going to Mum's either. No one can make me. They can't.

I fold the envelope carefully and tuck it away in my bag.

I'm starving. I forgot to take my lunch to school and I need the toilet really badly. I pull my Maths homework out and stare at it to distract myself. The fractions keep swirling on the page and turning into Amy's words.

They make my heart pound in my ears and my face and hands drip with sweat. *You're going on a train to your mum's! You have to go to your mum's! To your mum's!*

My eyes are prickly and blurry and I can't even see the numbers any more because they're swimming. I squeeze the tears away and stuff the fractions back in my bag. I get out my Geography homework and draw a huge volcano. I make loads of molten red lava gush out the top and spill down the sides. I draw loads of tiny little cars and houses, and miniature stick people running away. I make them all scream, with big howling mouths, like that painting called *The Scream* in my book. I draw loads of ash smoke billowing everywhere and blinding everyone and I draw a girl on a bench; alone, with all the hot lava and amber sparks whooshing towards her.

My legs are cold. I open the backpack, but it makes my tummy churn so I tug at the nylon straps and click the black buckles shut. If I don't read the letter and I don't look in the bag maybe it will all go away. Maybe it's really a dream and in a minute I'll go back home and Dad will be sighing on the sofa and Amy will be trying on her new stuff and everything'll be like normal.

My mum keeps prowling around my brain, lurking like a sharp-toothed shark. And what's weird is I can see everything from years ago as if it were yesterday, as if I had a TV on replay in my mind. There's Mum pulling on one arm, screeching, and Dad pulling on the other arm, sobbing, and I'm in the middle and only five. I'm just standing there with a blank face feeling invisible. No one even notices that they're tearing me in half like paper. And Beckett's just standing there trembling with his arms hanging long at his sides and his face turned whiter than the moon.

I wanted to go with Beckett so badly. But I couldn't leave Dad alone, could I? He looked so helpless and Mum made me feel so shaky and panicky inside. And then she spat in Dad's face and dropped my hand. She grabbed hold of Beckett and pulled him away. I wanted to run after him. I wanted to fly to Beckett. I wanted to hold on so tight and never let him go. And I tried to move my legs, I did, but they wouldn't move. They couldn't leave Dad standing there alone, looking so sad.

After I've finished colouring in the volcano I start

answering the questions.

1: What is the Ring of Fire?

The Ring of Fire is a volcanic chain surrounding the Pacific Ocean.

2: Where are volcanoes located?

Volcanoes are found along destructive plate boundaries, constructive plate boundaries and at hot spots in the earth's surface.

3:What are lahars and pyroclastic flows?

I know what those big words mean, but I can't be bothered to write the answer down. My mum's biting huge chunks out of my brain with her shark's teeth, blood dripping down her face. My tummy's grumbling. I try calling Dad again, and Amy. A plane roars overhead and it makes me think about them flying off. Where are they even *going*?

I pack my stuff up and start walking. I don't really think about where I'm going, but suddenly I'm standing at Grace's front door, which is painted smooth red and has a shiny brass lion's head knocker and letterbox. Yellow flowers nod in wooden boxes on the windowsill and tangles of white roses hang around the doorway like a big messy fringe. I stuff my nose in a creamy bloom and breathe in its perfume. It smells so beautiful. "Hi," I say, when Grace's mum opens the door. "Is Grace in?"

"Sorry, love," she says, "she's at her dad's tonight. You'll see her at school tomorrow."

"Oh," I say, hopping from one leg to another. "Sorry, I forgot."

I stand there like a dummy with my mouth hanging wide open. "Can I quickly use your bathroom, then? I'm desperate."

Grace's mum smiles and opens the door wide to let me in. I dump my bags in the hallway, race up the stairs and wee until there's not even one drop left inside me. I fold the flowery toilet paper round and round my hand and stroke its softness on my cheek. On my way back I peep into Grace's room and I wish I could slide into her bed and hide. I wish her mum could bring me some dinner up on a tray and puff the pillows so they're comfy. I wish she could climb in and watch a programme on Grace's pink telly with me.

"Bye, then," says Grace's mum, when I've picked up my bags.

I stare at her, a million words racing round my mind, thundering like horses.

"Can I have a biscuit, please?" I say.

Grace's mum laughs, then she gets the biscuit tin from the kitchen and lets me choose. "Take a couple," she says, "but don't go spoiling your tea."

I take two. My hand lingers in the tin. I should pull it out, I know, but it won't budge. My tummy's grinding like a peppermill.

"Oh, go on," she smiles, "take a handful, but don't tell your dad!"

She looks at me with these soft friendly eyes. She touches her hand on mine and I wish I could grab it and cling on like the roses round the door. I wish I could say something. I wish I could tell her.

"You OK, Gabriella?" she says. "You look, um…"

"I'm fine," I say, grabbing more biscuits. "Just starving after Games, that's all." I skip down the path very fast, away from her eyes and her questions. "Thanks for the biscuits, thank you, bye!"

Chapter 4

I walk around the park for ages, nibbling the biscuits, traipsing round and round. I watch the little kids on the swings, the boys on the skate ramps, the old people playing a really boring-looking game with lots of black shiny balls. I check that Dad's letter is still in my bag about seven hundred times. I think about Dad. I think about Mum. I think about Beckett and the stripy jumper he was wearing when he walked away in those faded jeans with the pink of his knee poking through the frayed rips.

"You all right, love?" a lady asks when I walk past the little café. "You've been marching about for ages. I keep on seeing you. Those bags look heavy."

"Errrrrm," I stutter, "yeah, I'm OK. I just feel like walking."

"Can't stop for a quick cupcake then?" she smiles. "I'm just about to shut up shop and I have one left, begging to be eaten."

"Errrrrm."

"Oh, go on," she says. "You can have it for free. If you don't tell, I won't tell, so long as you don't go spoiling your dinner. Don't want your mum chasing after me, do I?"

She hands me the cupcake. It's covered in pink icing with tiny red hearts.

"Thanks."

I take the cupcake and carry on walking. I lick the icing. I nibble the hearts. I sit on a bench and let the warm sun kiss me.

Maybe Mum's changed and things'll be different. Maybe if I do go there everything'll be OK. I probably won't even recognise Beckett and he definitely won't recognise me.

My tummy twists, that knotty nest of fear unravelling

and turning to snakes. But what if she hasn't changed? What if she blames me for everything that happened? What if she goes mad at me again? No one can make me go. *There isn't even anyone to make me.* I could disappear forever and no one would ever know.

I pull the letter out again and stare at it. I trace my finger over the shapes and my heart thunders. *Gabriella.*

Gabriella Midwinter. Beckett Midwinter. Dave & Sally Midwinter. Midwinter. Midwinter. Midwinter. Families are so silly.

I wiggle my finger under the flap and loosen the seal. I slide it all the way along until the envelope opens like a big white mouth and then I take a deep breath and pull the letter out. I try to hold it still enough to read, but my arms are juddering, and the paper is fluttering like a moth in my hands.

"Still here?" says the café lady, walking past.

I nod and stuff the letter in my pocket. "Thanks for the cake, it was lovely."

"You sure you're OK, sweetheart?" she asks, coming closer. "Nothing wrong is there?"

I shake my head.

"I'm meeting my dad here," I lie. "We're having a picnic before Parents' Evening. We're celebrating because my artwork is on display."

"Awww, that's lovely," she smiles. "Have a nice time. And good luck with Parents' Evening!"

I wish I was having a picnic with Dad. Instead, I find some nature stuff on the ground and make my own little tea party. I use buttercups for cups, a flat piece of wood for a table and a smooth round stone for a teapot. I bend little twigs to make a family, sit them all around and make tiny cakes and buns out of berries, and miniature green sandwiches from leaves.

There. Everyone's smiling. Everyone's happy and having fun. A pain swells up in my chest. I swallow it down and pick up my bags. I leave my twig family behind and hope a little girl finds them and has a play before the wind blows and scatters them across the grass.

I leave the park and walk up and down the streets, wondering what it would've been like if Dad actually *was* going to Parents' Evening to see my artwork and take photos of it on his phone.

Then I remember having a picnic with Grace and

her mum. We hired a canoe, paddled up the canal and then stopped when we were far away from everyone. It was all green shade and magical rays of sunlight bursting through. I couldn't believe it was real; it was like the paintings. We had egg sandwiches and crisps and chocolate cake and real orange juice with bits in, not squash. Grace's mum bought us white chocolate Magnum ice creams and we sat on the edge of the canal for hours, watching the boats float by and the moorhens nesting. We took off our sandals and dangled our feet in the freezing water and laughed.

Dad's letter is bashing about in my pocket, demanding attention. I walk and walk until the straps on the backpack start digging in again and my legs are achy and tired. And when I can't walk any more I find a bench, hunt in my school bag for my bottle and glug some water down. I find a warm, brave place in my heart, swallow down the big hard lump in my throat and pull the letter out. I stare at it, tracing my finger over the blue biro shapes looping across the page.

Dear Gabriella,

I know I should have told you, but I didn't know how. Amy and me are making a fresh start together and it's time for you to go and live with your mum. Amy thinks it'll be good for you to see her and Beckett. Here's some money for the train and for food while you're travelling. You're a big girl now. I know you'll be OK.

Mum's address is: 4, Macklow Street, Manchester. You'll be a nice little surprise!

Dad

I swallow hard. I pick the little scab on my arm. I trace my finger over the words again and again and again. I sit there for a lifetime, my heart thudding in my chest, waiting for the sun to go down, watching the wind lift litter from the path.

"Can I have a ticket to Manchester?" I say, to the man at the railway station.

He peers at me through the glass. "Single or return?"

"Single."

He taps away at the computer screen. He squints his

eyes to read. "Sorry, Miss," he says, "last train's already gone. You'll have to wait till morning."

I stare at him. "There must be something?"

He shakes his head and peers through the glass again. "Bit young to be travelling alone this time of night, aren't you?"

"Everyone says that. I'm just small for my age." And I'm not sure why, but suddenly I'm lying again.

The man nods and turns back to his computer. I wander away and press the green button on my phone and listen to Dad's voice seventeen times. I walk and walk and walk, until the town is hushed, until the sky grows dark, until there's no one else around except me walking and walking under a bright, bright moon.

Without noticing where I'm going I find myself standing in the shadows near Grace's house, like a thick elastic band has pulled me back here. I should knock on the door and tell her mum what's going on. But I'm scared she'll phone the police and get my dad in trouble for leaving me alone.

I slip down the alleyway between the houses, stumbling in the dark, counting the back gates until I find Grace's, number 58. I lean my arm over and slide the bolt open as quietly as I can. I can't swallow. I can't breathe. I think I might be sick.

I tiptoe through the garden towards the shed, feeling like a thief, avoiding the pond, careful not to clatter the swing. Grace's garden is washed with silvery moonlight and a soft golden glow spills from the house like honey, spreading across the lawn. It's quiet and still, except for the silhouetted leaves fluttering in the breeze and my heart hammering fast in my throat.

"Here, Kitty, Kitty," Grace's mum calls from the kitchen door, bashing a tin can with a spoon.

I freeze. I press myself against the shed door. Kitty leaps off the shed roof, on to the fence, and down to the ground with a pitter-patter thud.

"Come on, Kitty Kat," her mum calls again.

Kitty winds her soft furry body around my ankles. She nuzzles up close and purrs.

"Kitty Kat, come on."

I try pushing her gently away, towards the house, but she won't go, she just keeps on twirling around me.

"Suit yourself," says Grace's mum at last. "Out on the town are you, Kitty? Chasing mice?"

She puts the cat bowl down and then she stands and tips her head right back to gaze up at the stars. I have to stop myself from flying into her arms and telling her everything, from clinging on to her forever. I wish she'd stand there all night, with the halo glow of the kitchen light around her. I wish she'd walk into the darkness and find me and take charge.

Grace's mum shuts the door and turns the key. She snaps off the light, plunging the garden into dark silvery shadows of moonshine. I stoop down and pick Kitty up. I nuzzle my face in her fur.

"Go get your dinner, Kitty," I whisper, putting her back on the ground. "Go on, you'll be hungry." But she won't go and I just stand there, waiting.

When the clouds first roll in, soft glittery rain tumbles from the sky, but then the drops get bigger and wetter. I shelter under a tree and wait with my fringe dripping on to my cheeks, until all the upstairs lights go off. And when the house is totally quiet, I creak the shed door open and creep inside.

Kitty leaps on to the workbench sending tins of paint and bottles of stuff flying. I freeze. I hold my breath. I tremble. I wait for Grace's mum to come shouting into the garden in a panic to see what all the noise is about. I wish she would. I cross my fingers and toes and hope she won't.

The shed window is so grubby and full of cobwebs the moonlight can't get in. I drag my bags into the dry and shut the door. I run my hands over cold things, a lawnmower, garden tools, a metal bucket. I bash my knee pulling a sun lounger from the pile and I struggle to put it up.

I think about Blue Bunny and wonder if he's in my bag. I've never been to sleep without him before. I swallow hard, settle myself down and dig around in the backpack looking for his soft silky ears. I feel a hairbrush, a toothbrush, some scissors and scraps, a book and some clothes.

I dig deeper and deeper, then freeze when the low rumbling thunder rolls over me and bright white lightning cracks open the sky. I hold myself tightly as the storm rain lashes the window and drips through a crack.

And I squeeze my eyelids together.

To stop my tears from leaking out.

Chapter 5

I wake to the sound of the bin lorry munching and crunching on rubbish and for a moment I forget where I am. I stretch and yawn and blink. And then I see the lawnmower and the paint tins and feel Kitty's fur under my hands, and everything comes flooding back.

Amy. Dad. The letter. *Mum.*

A tiny spider dangles from a thread and Kitty bats it with her paw.

My throat squeezes tight.

What am I supposed to do now?

Do I just get on a train and find my mum and say, *"Hi, I hate you because you scared me to death when I was small, but I'm coming to live with you anyway because my dad, who I stayed with because I was so worried about leaving him alone, has just walked out on me!"*

And what does Dad think will happen next?

That she'll pull me into her arms and hug me and whisper, "Sorry darling," into my ear? Did he think she'd just sign me up for a new school and dance lessons with sparkly leotards and all that stuff and we'd live happily ever after like Grace?

That's the problem with Dad. He never thinks anything through. If he had, he wouldn't have let any of this happen. He'd have thought about me instead of Amy.

I take a sip of water from my bottle.

But what if Mum has changed? She might be really kind now. And what if... what if I find Beckett? What then? Will he know what to do?

I rub clear a little patch on the grubby glass window and watch a little robin pecking at the ground, trying to catch a juicy worm. I'm not hungry. My tummy has turned into this massive empty cave with seawater churning and sloshing inside. I wish I could see what's happening in Grace's house. I check my phone. I press the green button and hear it go straight through to Dad's answer phone. *"Hi, Dave here, I'm off on me hols, so don't leave a message as I won't be getting back to you anytime soon."* I don't try Amy's because my battery is running so low.

I wonder where they are now. Lying on some beach, or in a big soft hotel bed, or by a pool drinking cocktails? Amy's probably still shopping like mad, Dad's fingers shaking as he hands over the credit card because he knows he won't be able to pay the bill.

I wish I didn't care about him so much. I wish I could just rub him out of my life like he has me. I hate thinking about it all. It makes this big hard lump in my throat. Everything's spinning around like a fairground ride. It's creepy that no one knows where I am, that no one's missing me or worried that I've not come home.

I pull out my rough book and a pencil and sketch a picture of the robin and the worm. It's quite hard because the robin keeps bobbing about and the worm keeps wriggling. So I turn it into a surrealist picture by making the worm turn round and eat the bird.

Grace's mum opens the back door and smells of strong coffee and toast drift outside into the sunshine. If only I could sneak in and hide until she's gone to work. I'd run a big deep bath with bubbles and lie about and watch telly all day long.

"Kitty, Kitty, Kitty," she calls. "Where are you?"

I shove Kitty off my lap and force her outside. I hear the robin flap away.

"What were you doing all night, Kitty?" she says. "You didn't eat your tea! Catching birds were you?"

I hold my breath. I can't be found. She mustn't know. *Please find me!*

I decide to hide for a little while longer and then go to school as normal. I need to see Grace before I go to Manchester, just one last time.

I rub the sleep from my eyes, brush my hair and do my fractions homework. I re-read Dad's letter nine times even though I know it off by heart. I count my money, straighten everything up in the shed so it's just like I found it, pick up my things and creep outside. I keep my eyes on the house; scared Grace's mum will see me, hoping she's already gone to work.

It's weird being at school. I stuff my backpack at the back of the art cupboard so no one will see it, and shrug my shoulders when Mrs Evans mentions that Dad didn't make it to Parents' Evening. I feel different somehow, like I don't really belong here any more. Nothing at school seems important when you're worried about getting to Manchester and about what's going to happen when you get there. I'm not bothered about my homework. I don't even care about seeing my artwork on the wall.

"Doesn't it look great?" says Mrs Evans, standing next to me. "You should feel so proud of yourself, Gabriella."

I stare at my painting and shrug. Yesterday I was so excited about Grace's mum seeing it when she was here talking to the teachers. But today it's not important any more.

"Are you OK?" Mrs Evans says, glancing at me. "Look, tell your dad he can pop in any time he likes to see your work. It'd put some of the GCSE students' work to shame."

The word *shame* slides under my skin like a cold, wet fish, cringing inside me. I must have done something wrong. I must be a bad person for everyone in my life to leave me.

"You OK?" says Grace, staring at me while we're waiting for English to start. "You look like you've been dragged through a hedge backwards."

I'd like to tell her everything. A million words are fighting to get out of my mouth, but I don't really know where to start. We've been best friends for ages, Grace and me. She knows what cereal I like, what telly programmes I watch and that I'm really obsessed with art. She knows I think Will Thomas in Year 9 is cute and that I like white chocolate Magnums. But she doesn't know that my tummy scrunches up smaller than a walnut when people shout or that the shadow of my mum and the dark bruises she gave are always lurking behind me. She doesn't know that until Amy came along I'd been cooking tea for Dad and me every day for years.

"I'm OK," I say. "Just tired."

"How was Parents' Evening?" she asks, tearing a bright pink bubblegum and putting half in my mouth. "Everyone was really happy with me except Mr Chapman who said I talk too much! To you! Did he say that to your dad, too?"

"Yeah," I say, hearing more lies tumble out of me. "I told my dad that it's no wonder we talk because Mr Chapman is the most boring teacher in the world."

"My dad took me to Babington House for dinner," she says, "to celebrate Parents' Evening."

"My dad took me for a picnic in the park," I lie. "We had cupcakes and everything."

At break time I can't stand it any more. I've turned into a liar and I hate it. I think about leaving a note in Grace's locker or slipping one in her bag, but I don't want her to make a fuss. I don't want her to panic and get everyone searching, so I decide to tell her the truth.

Well, kind of the truth. Half of the truth.

"I have to go away," I say. "To go and be with my mum."

"What d'you mean?" she cries. "You haven't seen

your mum in years!"

"I know, but my dad thinks it's time I went to see her. It's all arranged."

I dig my nails in my palm. My lies slip sliding through me like threads of stringy cheese. "He's driving me up there today," I say. "I don't have any choice."

Grace's eyes flash open wide.

"What do you mean, today?" she shrieks. "You can't just go! You're supposed to be coming for a sleepover at the weekend. We're going swimming, it's all arranged! We're best friends, Gabriella! Why didn't you tell me? I knew something was wrong, I knew it! I knew it wasn't just because you were tired!"

"I… I didn't know before," I say. "He only decided last night, all of a hurry. I wanted to tell you in English, but I didn't know what to say. I think Amy's got something to do with it. I don't want to go, Grace, but I have to."

"Do the teachers know?" she says.

"Yes," I lie. "He told them at Parents' Evening. It's OK, Grace, we'll stay in touch, I promise. You can come and visit me and stuff, we can still chat online and text.

And if it doesn't work out I'll be back."

"But what about me?" she shrieks. "What about us?"

"We'll still be *us*," I say. "Nothing can change that, Grace, not ever."

"But you'll be so far away. You can't just go!"

"I'm sorry, Grace," I say, picking up my bag. "I'm really, really sorry, but there's nothing I can do."

She glares at me and eats her Wagon Wheel in three bites without sharing.

Chapter 6

"Can I have a train ticket to Manchester, please?" I say to the lady at the ticket office.

"Which one?" she says. "There's more than one station in Manchester, my love."

"Errrr, I, eerrmm."

"Just the main one?" she says, squinting at the computer screen. "Manchester Piccadilly?"

I nod. "Errr, yes, that's right. That's the one."

"You're in luck, and you've only got a twenty-minute wait," she says, glancing at her watch. "You'll see you need to change at Bristol Temple Meads, OK? You've only got one change, so it shouldn't be too tricky.

Someone meeting you at the other end, are they?"

I nod again and force a big smile on my face. "Yes,' I say, "my mum'll be waiting for me."

"OK, then," she smiles. "Good girl, you take care."

I find my way to the platform on legs made of jelly. I wish the ticket lady hadn't been so kind; it makes things worse. It was the same with the lady in the park café and Grace's mum. They make me feel weak and small, like I might just buckle over all at once and cry. They make me work extra hard at looking normal and keeping a smile drawn across my face.

I lug my bags on to the platform, find my way to the ladies' toilets and lock myself in a cubicle. It's smelly with stale wee and disinfectant and lady's perfume is still clinging to the walls like paint. But I like it in here because I'm invisible. No one's staring or asking questions.

A nutty ball of anger about Grace is bothering me. I don't want to be angry with her, but it's travelling around me looking for a place to settle. I don't know why I'm even going to Manchester. I'm not going to live with my mum, so why am I even getting on the train?

I sit on the toilet seat and pick the scab on my arm while I think. I need to stop picking it really because every time it gets better I start picking and picking again, making it bleed. Amy's words ring loud in my brain. *"Stop picking, Miss Flappy Ears, you'll pick yourself to death at this rate!"*

Maybe I should go back to the park and talk to the cupcake lady. I could tell her how worried I am that my dad'll get into trouble. Then maybe she won't call the police; maybe she'll just take care of me until I'm old enough to get a job. We wouldn't have to tell anyone; we could pretend she was my auntie or something. We could say my dad had to go away to work. Even Grace wouldn't have to know, or school, and I could go back in tomorrow like normal.

I could help her out in the café at weekends. I could make cupcakes. I'm sure I'd be really good at cupcakes. Maybe I should've told Mrs Evans, she would definitely know what to do. I could sleep in the art cupboard on cushions and clean the art room up for her every evening and she could bring me food. It might be OK.

My hands tremble as I open my backpack and peer

inside. I pull out some jeans, my favourite blue top with the shiny ribbon bit around the neck and my fake leopard-print jacket. I take off my uniform, yesterday's knickers and socks and slip the clean stuff on, wobbling on one foot, trying to miss a little puddle of water on the floor. I wish I could have a hot shower, or a flannel wash, or even baby wipes. I balance on the toilet seat, pull on my Converse and lace them up. My mouth feels dry; there's this big knotty lump in my throat. At least I won't stand out so much wearing jeans. I might look old enough that no one will wonder if I'm skiving off school.

I dig my hand deep into my backpack, squirrelling and searching again. Dad knows how much I need Blue Bunny; he knows I can't sleep without him. But what if Amy packed my bag? She said I was a baby for still having a bunny at my age. But what does she know about anything?

My hand slices through my stuff, my fingers scrabbling through the rough wool of a jumper, the softness of my hoody, the hard knobbly socks rolled up together. I run my fingers round some books, pushing my hand deeper. Hope filling me like stars on a cold black night. My fingertips travel the rough sequined fabric of my diary with the bendy up corner, the shiny plastic of my strawberry pencil case, the soft cotton brush of my knickers. And down at the bottom with all the gritty bits and tissues and sweet wrappers I find a silky label and a love-soft ear. I pull Blue Bunny out and I can't stop grinning. I kiss him on the little heart Beckett drew on his chest when he was ten and stroke the silky label against my lip. Then my hand starts searching again; my mind starts flapping.

What about my photo? What about my photo of Beckett?

I open the cubicle door, and avoiding the puddle of water, hold my backpack upside down and clatter the mish-mash, click-clack of colourful stuff on to the floor. My fingers sift through it like baby bloodhounds, hunting. What did they do with my photo? *Beckett, where are you?*

Beckett's not here. They forgot him. Probably threw him out with all the other stuff or left him for Mrs McKlusky to sweep away. The little glass frame is probably cracked and cutting Beckett's face, making scars. Fat tears roll down my cheeks without me even knowing they were coming. My lips pull tight and tremble.

I stare at my face in the cloakroom mirror, watching it turn into an ugly gargoyle. I press my hands on my cheeks and open my mouth, pulling my jaw down, letting out a silent scream that I hope someone, somewhere, will hear. Then I splash cold water on my face, scrub my hands with soap and brush my hair. I fumble to find my toothbrush. I load it up with toothpaste and feel the cool minty flavour zing through me, setting my gums on fire. I stuff everything in my backpack and fill my water bottle from the tap. I stare at my face in the mirror again, shooing the gargoyle away, willing my lips to smile so that no one will see the volcano erupting inside me.

It's weird being on the train alone. I feel like everyone's watching, like they all know what's happening to me. Like what Dad has done and how bad I am is written over my face in loud, loopy handwriting. They keep staring like cats, slyly out of the corners of their eyes.

I stuff my backpack under my seat and put my school bag on the one next to me. I cross my fingers and toes, hoping that no one will come and sit down. I don't want their questions. I don't want anyone finding out and telling on Dad.

I wonder where he is now? I wonder what he's doing? I wonder when his wedding actually *is*? If Amy had been nicer I could've been a bridesmaid. I would've done it for Dad if she'd asked.

What did I do to make everyone leave?

"Excuse me, my lovely," says a man with snowy dandruff falling from his head. "Don't mind if I do?"

He nods at my school bag, starts nudging his knees into the space and his bum on to the seat. My tummy swirls. The skin on my face pulls tight. I do mind if he does, actually. I wish everyone would just leave me alone.

"Errr," I say, lying, pulling my school bag on my lap. "OK."

He slides on to the seat and puffs huge gusts of rotten egg breath in my face.

"Lovely weather," he smiles, jiggling his knee up and

down. "Off somewhere nice?"

I stare at him without answering and hug my school bag close. I'm not going to talk to him. I'm not going to say one word. I'm not stupid enough to talk to strangers who make my tummy flip and something ice cold twist in my skin. I turn and look out the window, heat spreading on my cheeks like the sun, and make myself invisible. Fading back so he can't see me; disappearing so he won't ask questions.

"No school then?" he says, butting his big beak over my shoulder. "You don't look old enough to be out alone this time of day."

I keep my ears closed and watch the yellow stone houses flash past the window and the fresh green fields and the trees. I watch the white clouds wisp by, pressing my face on the cool glass, feeling the clack and the screech of the train wheels turning and spinning inside me.

"You're a quiet one, then," he says, leaning into me, puffing egg breath near my nose. "Shy, are yer?"

I look at people's washing lines and try to peer inside their homes. I count the sheds, the bikes, the trampolines and the barbecues.

"I'm Colin," he says, jiggling his knee again. "You don't need to be shy of me. I don't bite."

His knee jiggle turns into an egg-breath shake of laughter. He pushes in a little bit closer. I press harder on the window glass until my face is flattened.

"Woof, woof!" he chuckles, nudging me with his fat elbow. "Get it! Get it! Woof! Woof! I don't bite!" He buckles over with laughter, slapping his hand on his thigh.

When we get to Bristol Temple Meads I grab my backpack and run, fighting my way through the crowds. So many platforms. So many trains. So much noise. I stare at my ticket, my eyes blurring, my mind spinning.

"Need a hand, my love?" says dandruff man, blustering up to me. "Show me your ticket then, show Colin where you're going, and I'll help you."

I keep my eyes on the ground, on a discarded leaflet for *The Lion King* at the Hippodrome, a wall of rotten egg smell hanging between us. I stuff my ticket deep into my pocket, far away from his eyes and pick up my bags. I weave through the thick crowd, quick as a needle, sideways and in circles to escape him.

"Can you tell me which platform I need, please?" I ask the lady at the information point, handing her my ticket.

She stares at it, then at her computer screen, slowly running her chipped nail-varnish finger down the line of lit-up words. I scan the station for Colin with Mrs McKlusky's sharp eagle eyes, my ears burning, my heart thumping its fat hard fist on my ribs. "Platform five," she says, pointing. "That way."

I move quickly through the swarm of people pushing to get to their trains, my eyes constantly checking. I can't let Colin see which train is mine; he mustn't know I'm going to Manchester.

Chapter 7

Once I'm on the train I stuff my bags in the overhead thing and hide in the toilet for years, Colin prowling in and out of my thoughts like a panther. I didn't see him get on the train, but I can't take any chances. Anyone knows he's the kind of man to be avoided.

I need to think about my bags. I can't carry both of them forever. I wash my hands in the grubby grey sink with the pink liquid soap that smells of the little sick room at school. And a new idea thumps through me, the thrill of it swelling up inside. *No one's looking for me.* Dad and Amy won't know if I get to Mum's or not. No one minds. No one cares. I'm free to do what I want.

Grace and I have dreamt about this kind of freedom under the covers at night, curled up all legs and arms and hot breath, whispering secrets, making plans. We'd skip everywhere in the world together clapping our hands, with skinny arms linked behind our backs, doing anything we liked. We'd be totally invincible, having adventures with *Swallows and Amazons* and *The Famous Five* and *Mallory Towers* and *Harry Potter* in Grace's soft room with the smell of her mum's rose perfume still lingering on the stairs.

I am free now. I can do what I want. And I'm not going to my mum's. Not ever!

I pull my phone out and text Grace. I feel bad about not telling her the truth.

Sorry I had to go. I miss u already. xxx

After a few seconds she texts back.

The teachers r looking for u. ur dad didn't tell them u were leaving. everyone's freaking out. where r u gabs?

My cheeks thrum with the heat of lying to my best friend, but I can't tell her what's happening.

I told u, I'm ok. I am going to my mum's. love u xxx

I switch off my phone. I don't want those kinds of

worries crashing about in my brain. I can't think about what's going on at school or worry about Grace's feelings. I pull the leftover money from my pocket and count it out, unfolding the crumpled note neatly and making a shining tower of coins. A shiver snakes through me. I can't have many adventures on this money. It won't last forever, and then what? In my mind Mum's shark teeth gnash at me, her hand comes flying towards my face. Colin's sweaty snow-face-egg-breath sneers. I can't go to Mum's. I can't. I won't!

"Are you all right in there?" a lady calls, banging on the door with her fist. "You've been in there for ages!"

I wipe my hands on the rough blue paper towel and throw it in the bin with the flappy lid. "Er, sorry," I shout, battling with the tricky door lock. "I, er, erm."

"The toilets are for everyone's use," she snaps. "You can't just hog them like that. I've a mind to report you if you do it again."

Back in my seat I check my watch. I still have nearly three hours until I get to Manchester Piccadilly. I pull my school bag down from the overhead thingy and rummage through it again to see what I can get rid of.

I take out my exercise books and I flick through them. It was a waste of time doing all that work now no one's even going to read it or mark it. I find a red pen and go through the pages one by one giving myself A* for everything. I write things like *Excellent work, Gabriella,* and *I'm astonished by your brilliance, Gabriella,* in the margin.

I stack the books in a pile and hold up my PE kit, stretching the big blue knickers as wide as they can go, letting the nylon silky top slither over my hand. I don't need any of it. I don't do PE any more. I don't go to school. I'm as free, free, free as a bird.

I pick everything up and bump past a lady lost in her laptop. She sighs like it's the end of the world, like I might be arrested for disturbing her work. I walk up the train with my heart thumping, my hands shaking, and lock myself in a different toilet. I tear off the front covers of my exercise books that have my name written on and flush them down the loo, page by page. I draw black pen scribbles on the labels on my uniform until my name disappears then I stuff them in the bin with my books. I'm nameless, invisible.

Back in my seat, with the laptop lady huffing and puffing and tutting beside me, I get out some drawing things. I doodle some poodle dogs balancing on a tightrope, some pretty flowers climbing up a wall, a long, long line of tiny trains going nowhere. I doodle Dad's face and then cross it out, then feel guilty, so I draw it again. I doodle shark teeth, gnashing and blood dripping. I doodle Chang's fish swimming round and round in circles and Grace's mum's front door with its rosy fringe. The laptop lady smells like Grace's mum. Her hands are nutmeg brown with sparkling rings and bright red shiny nails. I don't want her asking questions, but I'd quite like her to nod at me or say hello or smile instead of being so stressy and just tapping on her keyboard. When the train stops at Birmingham New Street station, she snaps her laptop shut, stuffs it in her black leathery bag and makes a dash for the door.

The world and everything rushing past makes me feel a little bit dizzy and sick. I rest my head back in my seat and close my eyes. I wish I had a blanket. I wish I were brave enough to pull Blue Bunny out and snuggle him in front of everyone. My mum swims round my brain, her big teeth glinting. Colin lurches in front of my eyes, flaking dandruff all over me, puffing great huge gusts of eggy breath in my face. I grip the arm of the seat, open my eyes in a flash and start checking, searching the carriage for Colin's face or Mum's.

When we get to Wolverhampton a teenage boy with floppy blond hair, wearing a T-shirt saying *No Fear*, drops into the seat that the laptop lady left behind. He tucks his skateboard between his knees, plugs himself into his iPod and starts munching on a hot cheesy pasty. I'm so hungry my tummy is growling. I haven't eaten since the cupcake in the park. I feel the money in my pocket, run the coins through my fingers and rustle the paper note. I'll just spend the coins and save the note for later, for emergencies.

I find a fresh page on my pad and draw the kind of Mum I'd really like. She has soft, smooth hair and a gentle smile and lovely straight teeth. I put her in a green and pink flowery dress with one of those little cardigan things that Grace's mum wears, in matching green. I give her sparkly earrings that twinkle, and tuck a big pink rose behind her ear. If I could turn my picture into one of those scratch and sniff ones she'd smell of roses and apple crumble.

When the refreshment trolley comes past I buy myself a Snickers bar. I hold it for a while, just looking at it, then I tear open the paper and take tiny little bites, letting the creamy chocolate melt slowly. I look at the boy out of the corner of my eye and think about Beckett. I wonder if he has an iPod and a skateboard? I wonder if he's got a T-shirt that says *No Fear*? I wonder if he likes cheesy pasties best or meaty ones?

A lump grows in my throat; a tiny tear leaks out of my eye. I swallow hard. I pull my phone out of my bag and press the green button five times. *"Hi, Dave here, I'm off on me hols, so don't leave a message as I won't be getting back to you anytime soon."* "Dad!" I whisper. "Dad, where are you?"

When we get to Stockport the skateboard boy gets up and leaves. I check my watch. My tummy squeezes and bitter-tasting sick rises up to my throat. Ten minutes left until we get to Manchester Piccadilly. I pull Dad's letter out of my pocket and trace my fingers over his words.

Mum's address is Macklow Street, Manchester. You'll be a nice little surprise!

I try calling him again, but this time I don't even get to hear his voice because my phone battery dies.

As the train slows down, the metal wheels screech on the tracks and my heart gallops fast in my ears. Everyone looks up from their laptops, books, phones and iPods, all blinky-eyed and surprised. They fill up the aisle with coffee breath, grabbing for bags, pressing to reach the exit; checking the time, foot tapping, shuffling, pulling on jackets, chattering. They all have somewhere to go.

If I could melt into the seat I'd stay here forever. I fold up Dad's letter and stuff it safely in my pocket. I pull my backpack off the overhead thing, put my pencil case and paper inside and tuck my empty school bag under the seat. Swirling octopus tentacles of fear are moving inside me, a million difficult questions are raining on my mind. *What am I going to do? Where am I going to go? Who is going to take care of me?*

I pin myself to my seat while the train hisses to a halt, the doors clunk open and everyone hurries away.

"You all right there, pet?" asks a lady pushing a trolley

full of cleaning stuff.

"Errm, er, yes," I say, getting up. "Sorry, I must have fallen asleep. I'm just going."

Manchester Piccadilly station is huge, and thousands of people are swarming like bees. I stand in the middle under a long shaft of bright light shining through the glass ceiling, my head swimming with echoing sound. I lean against a wall, it's cold and hard on my back, and I watch a million feet trample past me.

I whisper to no one, *"Hello, I'm Gabriella. Can someone tell me what to do next, please?"*

I pick the scab on my arm until it bleeds then lick the metallic-tasting blood away.

I've never thought about God or any of that stuff before. Dad said it was all a load of rubbish: "Codswalloping tosh and brainwashing nonsense for people who can't think for themselves." Amy sings Christmas carols in the shower and that hymn that goes *Abide with me* because it reminds her of her nan's funeral. The idea of someone like God watching over me feels nice. It lulls my scared feelings to sleep, so I look up to heaven and try out a prayer.

"Dear God, please tell me what to do. Amen."

I stand there for ages, waiting for something to happen and wonder if God has angels with huge pure white wings, writing prayers down as they drift up through the clouds. I wonder if he'll answer, if he'll send a deep, dark rumble of thunder, or a bright white crack of lightning, to let me know he's heard? Maybe I'll hear his big deep voice booming out over the top of the loudspeaker lady who's saying which trains are coming and going.

"Hello, Gabriella Midwinter," he'll say. *"You need to turn left at the Costa coffee stall where your dream Mum and Dad will be waiting there for you, ready to take you off to your cosy new home. And Beckett will be there too and he'll know what to do and you'll all live happily ever after."*

I peer at the faces passing by, searching for a special sign from God. But maybe Dad's right; maybe it is all just a load of old codswallop.

Amy's nan's song plays round and round in my mind.
Abide with me;
fast falls the eventide;

the darkness deepens;
Lord with me abide.
When other helpers fail and comforts flee,
Help of the helpless,
O abide with me.

Amy had a lovely voice. That was the only nice thing about her. I sing the song under my breath, hoping someone will hear.

Chapter 8

An older teenage girl with hair that curls around her face like bubbles, and smudged make-up round her eyes comes and stands right near me. She pulls a guitar out of its case, drops a felt hat on the ground and starts singing in a voice smoother than chocolate. Her guitar strings dance on the air, the notes echoing through the great glass hall, making the tiny hairs on the back of my neck tingle. I slide a little closer. I'd like to hide in her bubbly hair, slide into her hat, or sit inside her guitar with all that music swirling around me.

Passersby stop for a minute to listen. They throw money into her hat, their faces breaking into smiles.

Like she's this amazing cool waterfall tumbling down on their hot and busy day. The girl sings on and on and I stand there, listening, searching through the crowd of faces for Beckett, waiting for something to happen.

When the girl finishes singing and leaves the station I make my way along the road. The streets are thundering with honking cars. Diesel fumes hover in a mist above the tarmac and scorch the back of my nose. Everyone's jostling. Everyone's pushing. The trams are squealing. I just keep walking, pretending I know where I'm going. Up and down the maze of streets, weaving through the crowds and past the shops and all the time searching for Beckett's face.

I stop near a crowd gathered round a man with tattoos, wearing short jeans and no top and big black boots. He's standing on a box juggling lemons; three, four, five of them spinning yellowy, high through the air. Then he does this dance and he sings something funny and everyone claps and laughs. And when he spins around I see them. These long, black angel wings tattooed on his back that somehow thrum inside me making my hands travel to the place on my back where wings might grow. I pull out my pad and stand there with a pencil in the middle of it all, drawing the spinning lemons, shading in the silky wings.

Further along there's two people covered in silver paint with silver ivy looped round their heads. Everyone's watching in silence, holding their breath because you can't really tell if they're real people or statues. And it makes me want to go over and tickle them or pinch them to see if they'll move. Music soaring to the sky is coming from a man playing a huge instrument that looks a bit like a xylophone. He's holding four sticks and he's swinging and hammering them so fast they look like a blur.

I walk on through the maze of colour and sound, past stalls with smells rising from them that make me think of Chang's takeaway place with the little fish swimming around. And suddenly this huge grey tower looms over me with a sign saying *Manchester Cathedral*. I walk faster, like the elastic band is pulling me again.

Inside the Cathedral I feel smaller than a mouse as I creep forward and slide into a seat. I close my eyes and a thick cloak of silence drapes around me. I slip my

Converse off and wriggle my toes to give them air. I move my shoulders round and round in wheels like we do in PE to relax them. I could stay in the Cathedral forever, with its black stone pillars and all the people walking about, looking at the big cross on the altar, whispering private prayers to God.

A man stops and stifles a sneeze. He pulls a white handkerchief out of his pocket and blows his fat purple nose. The huge stained-glass windows bend the sunlight, bathing us all in vivid rays of colour that turn my hand blue. I slip my Converse back on and walk around with my neck craned back, looking at the high-up, huge domed ceilings, thinking that the famous painter Michelangelo would've liked to visit here too. Grace's mum would love to see the nave, shining gold like the inside wrapper of a chocolate bar.

There's this little stand full of candles flickering in the soft breeze. There's a pile of them, still fresh and white and new, still waiting to be lit. I watch the people put coins in the box then light a candle and pray. I watch the little flames burn brightly. I want to light one so badly I can hardly keep my hands in my lap. I watch

what everyone does, waiting until they've drifted away
and when it's my turn, with a trembling hand, I light a
candle and pray.

"Dear God,
Please, help me!
Amen."

I drop a coin in the box and sit near the candle,
watching the blue and yellow flame quiver. I listen hard
for God, waiting for something to happen.

"Hello," a lady says, shuffling in the seat next to
mine. "It's not the most beautiful of cathedrals, is it?
But still, I think it's lovely."

I look at her, the muscles in my face twitching. "Err,
I just," I say, pointing to the candle, "is it OK?"

She laughs in a whisper. "Of course it's OK," she
smiles. "I just came over to let you know we're closing
up now for the night. Time to go home. But please feel
free to come back, anytime you like."

Outside, my body is as heavy as lead. I wander round
the Cathedral and lean against the hard stone wall,
crumbling the cement under my fingertips, watching
it fall to the ground like powdery snow. I sit on a

bench and swing my legs backwards and forwards. I pull out my sketchbook and design a whole new range of Converse sneakers with miniature turtles on them. I draw twenty little candles in a row and a cross with Jesus nailed to it, wearing that thorny ring thing on his head. I listen to my tummy rumble with hunger.

I pull out Dad's letter and read it again.

4 Macklow Street, Manchester. You'll be a nice little surprise!

Maybe I *should* go to Mum's and spy on her house until I see Beckett. I chew the end of my finger for a while, thinking, catching the little strips of skin between my teeth.

I head back to the train station and look at the big map of Manchester. I trace my finger along the streets until I find where Macklow Street is and write the directions to her house on my hand in lime-green felt pen. I go into a shop, pick up a packet of prawn cocktail crisps and dangle it between my finger and thumb. I stare for years at the juicy sandwiches on display.

"You buying, or what?" says the man behind the

counter. "Because if you're not you can put my crisps down!"

"I do want them," I tell him. "I was just thinking."

I pull myself away from the sandwiches and hand over the money for the crisps. "I was just thinking," I say. "I wasn't doing anything wrong."

When I get near Mum's my insides twist up in a knot and the crisps turn to sand in my mouth. I can't believe I'm actually looking at her house, at where she lives. I can't stop thinking about Beckett and the fact that he might actually be inside. I stay close to the fence on the other side of the road, my heart pounding, the tips of my ears burning. And when I'm almost opposite her front door I tuck myself in between a wheely bin and a broken fence to watch.

I stand there for ages with an annoying fly buzzing around my head and TV sounds blaring out at me. A few big boys scuff past, sipping from cans, kicking stones along the road, shouting. A whiff of sizzling sausages wafts from an open kitchen window, teasing my nose. I stay behind the fence, watching my mum's front door, waiting for Beckett to appear.

And I'm just about to give up when a man on a big black motorbike roars up and screeches to a halt outside Mum's door. He swings his leg over and hops off the bike. I freeze. *Beckett!* My heart crashes around like a wasp in a jar. The man tugs at his helmet and slips it over his head. His hair is a big messy hedge that trails down his face to make a dark bushy beard. His boots are huge. I can't see his face properly; I can't see how old he is. I squint hard to work out if the boy Beckett in my photograph could've grown into this big hairy man, or if this man is just too old. He walks up to the door, pulls out a key and puts it in the lock. I hold my breath.

"What you looking at?"

I jump and look down to see a small boy with a yellow bunny hanging out of his fist, standing right by me.

"Nothing," I say.

"Liar," he says, sucking the bunny ear while he speaks. "You're watching our place."

"I'm not," I say, picking up my backpack to leave. "I was just resting for a minute." I hold up my bag. "See, it's heavy."

"You robbing?" he says, picking a scab on his nose.

"No!" I say. "I told you already, I was resting!"

The boy shrugs, hops on his scooter and starts moving round and round in tight circles, keeping his eyes glued to me.

"Do you know that man who got off the bike?" I whisper.

The boy narrows his eyes. "Why?"

"Just wondered."

"S'me dad," he says, frowning. "No one special."

My heart sinks. Maybe Mum doesn't even live here any more. Maybe Dad got it wrong.

"D'you know someone called Beckett?" I hiss.

The boy's eyes grow as huge as saucers. "No, I don't, I don't know anyone like that!" He shakes his head hard, stuffs the bunny ear in his mouth and wheels round and round, pumping his knee like mad. And I'm just about to leave when Mum's front door swings open and a sour sick taste rises up in my throat.

"Connor!" Mum screeches. "Get in now, will you? Tea's ready!"

She's holding a toddler girl who is struggling to get

out of her arms.

"You wanna smack, Jayda?" Mum yells, clamping the little girl's chubby leg with her arm. The girl stops moving and shakes her head. "Then keep still, will you?"

Mum's screech cuts through me like a shark's black fin cuts through the sea. The boy looks up and blinks. He picks at a scab on his knee.

"Gotta go," he says, scooting off. "That's me mam."

Chapter 9

Even though it's closed and I know I won't be allowed back inside I run back to the Cathedral, pumping my legs hard, my body a trembling jelly of fear. Old memories and dark shadowy images of Mum's slapping hand chase me like an evil old shark rising from the depths of dangerous waters. She hasn't changed. *I knew it!* I knew she wouldn't!

I dig in my backpack for my sketchbook, find a pencil and draw the Cathedral and seven birds flying overhead. I draw my mum's big screechy face and a motorbike and a huge hairy beard and a scooter and a small boy with a yellow bunny. I draw a tiny girl with bubbly curls, struggling in Mum's big, hard hands. Tears choke up in my throat and press on the back of my nose. How couldn't I have known that I have a new brother *and* a sister? Why didn't anyone *tell* me?

I sit for ages, longing for Grace's shed and her mum with the halo glow of honey-coloured light spilling from her house. I think about my bed and wish I were curled up inside my rosebud duvet, far away from here, with Dad's TV programmes blaring away in the other room.

I've never really thought about my bed before. In the past 24 hours I've lost my bed, my home, my dad, my school and my best friend. Grace is a million miles from here, on another planet. My heart clenches up like a fist. All I have now is Mum and her hairy boyfriend and my new brother and sister. And all I want is *Beckett*.

I sip some water, careful not to drink too much because I don't know when I'll be able to fill my bottle up again. I look at my watch. Today is lasting forever. I find my scissors and some glue and sweet wrappers and start making beautiful things. I snip at little coloured cellophane bits. I fold some paper up loads of times and snip, snip, cutting little holes. When I open it up it's like a snowflake pattern and I stick the coloured bits over the holes to make a stained-glass window.

The evening sun rests a warm hand on my cheek and makes long dark shadows on the grass. A huge black dog bounds over, wagging its tail like a mad thing. I put my arms around its neck and look into its eyes. Its owner whistles and it bounds off with its long fluffy tail brushing the grass like a broom.

I turn the stained-glass window into a card and hold it up to the light so bright rainbows shine in my eyes. I write *Happy Birthday* inside, make a lovely envelope and wonder how much money I could get for it. I think about the picture I made with Beckett waving up at me and how I'd like to put stained-glass windows on that house to make it more beautiful.

When the sun goes down I count nine stained-glass cards and get the same warm feeling inside when Mrs Evans told me about my artwork being on display. I walk round the outside of the Cathedral eight and a half times wondering where I could sell them. I huddle near the entrance. Even though there's no one inside and I know the huge door is locked, I'm sure I can hear organ music playing inside and a child's crystal clear voice soaring up to the stars.

I walk up and down the road avoiding the cracks. I walk round and round and round. I sit on the steps near an old black and white pub and stare at the plates of left-over food on the tables outside. I yawn and touch the place on my back where angel wings would grow. I take off my Converse and wriggle my hot, throbbing toes.

"Quick," says a teenage girl with pink stripy hair. She grabs my wrist and pulls me away. "You can't hang around here."

"Why?" I say, struggling to get my bag on my back and stand up at the same time. "What's the problem?"

She flicks her eyes upwards as I stuff my Converse back on my feet. "That's the problem," she hisses. "CCTV cameras. You have to avoid them otherwise they'll find you!"

"Who'll find me?" I ask as she strides away pulling me with her.

"I don't know," she says, raising her eyebrows.

"Whoever's looking for you. If the police get you they'll take you in, send you back home or off to care. It'll all be over."

We duck into a quiet alley and stop to catch our breath.

"What would the police want with me?" I say, swirling with panic. "I haven't done anything wrong."

"They're always on the look-out for runaways," she says. "They want to get rid of us. They want to clean the streets up so we don't spoil everything. But follow me, I'll show you where's safe."

I kick the kerb.

"You don't have to," I say, folding my arms. "I'm OK, I'm just looking for my brother."

The girl's deep blue eyes search my face. "What's his name?" she smiles. "What's your name? I'm Henny."

"Beckett," I sniff, "and I'm Gabriella, Gabriella Midwinter. Do you know him?"

Henny folds her arms across her chest and leans back against the wall, thinking.

"No," she says at last, shaking her stripy head. "Never heard of him."

"He's lived here for seven years," I say. "He has brown

curly hair and he's nineteen. You must've seen him."

She laughs, twirling her finger around a strand of pink hair. "Manchester's a big place," she says. "You hungry, kitten?"

"A bit," I whisper, "but you don't have to bother."

"S'no bother," she says, dragging me by my sleeve. "I'll show you."

The smell of fish and chips and kebab drifts up the road and teases my nose. My tummy flips and turns. My money! I can't spend it! Not on food. Not on food for Henny as well.

"I'm all right," I say, pulling away and adjusting my bag. "I'm not hungry, not really."

Henny looks me up and down. "Liar," she says. "You're starving, it's written all over your face. You got money?"

I stare at the pavement. I shake my head, my lie wriggling through me like a worm.

"You're a really bad liar," she says. "Didn't anyone ever tell you your nose turns red when you lie?"

My hand flies up to my nose. My face burns ketchup red.

"I don't want your money," she says, looking offended. "I'm just trying to help. I don't know why I bother sometimes, but I guess they don't call me Henny for nothing."

I look up, confused.

"Listen," she says, "I saw you go up and down the street like a tramp, round and round, sitting out there in the open. It's not safe, the cameras and police and pervs and stuff."

She leans in close and whispers instructions in my ear.

"See, it's easy," she says, taking my bag and stepping back. "You just have to look all big eyed and innocent, kitten."

Henny winks and slips round the corner. My heart flips and bangs in my chest.

"Err... erm, my mum didn't come back home after work," I say to the red-faced man behind the fish and chip counter, "and me and my little brothers are starving. Any chance you could spare us some chips?"

The man pierces me with his jet-black eyes. "Clear

off," he snaps. "You kids are all the same. Go on! Clear off! Something for nothing, all of you."

I stand firm, my voice getting stronger, my lie getting bigger.

"I'm not lying," I say, "honest. My brothers are crying they're so hungry. I'll drop the money off tomorrow. I'll get it from my mum when she gets home."

"I said, clear off!" he shouts, so loud his words almost blow me over.

A tall man in a smart grey suit and blue stripy shirt steps forward. "Look," he says, jangling change in his pocket. "I haven't got time for all this. Give her what she wants and I'll pay."

I look up at him with big fluttering eyes, just like Henny said.

"Thank you," I say. "Thank you very much."

He keeps his eyes away from mine and he stares at the fish counter, jangling his change in his pocket again, silently nodding.

I skip outside, my arms full of steaming chips, feeling full to the brim with pride. I search for Henny. I walk up and down looking for her.

"Henny!" I call. "Look, I got them! I got loads for us to share!"

I pace up and down, craning my neck, straining my eyes.

"Henny? Where are you?"

And above the slamming, thrumming, clattering sounds of the night-time streets my heart drops to my tummy like a stone.

I gave her my bag.

I gave her my bag!

She has *everything*.

Chapter 10

"Ta-daah!" squeals Henny, jumping out of a dark doorway, throwing her arms open wide. "First rule, kitten, be careful who you trust, especially with your stuff."

She hands me my bag. My eyes brim over with tears, which I wipe on my sleeve as we walk along silently, sharing chips that stick in my throat like twigs.

"Are you angry with me?" she laughs. "Didn't scare you, kitten, did I?"

"No!" I lie. "I'm not a baby! I knew you hadn't gone! Not really!"

I stuff more chips in my mouth, kick a stone and

practise that poem about the dead soldier we had to learn for English, over and over inside my head.

After a while we come to this huge multi-storey car park. Henny drags me inside to find a huddle of kids laughing and cheering at three boys racing shopping trolleys up and down. "Whhhoooooooooooooo!" squeals one of the boys, skidding his trolley in and out of the cars.

"Ekkkkkkkkkkkkkk," screeches another, almost scratching the side of a big blue truck.

A girl with a ghost-white face wearing a jumper too thick for this weather starts chanting, "DARE! DARE! DARE!"

The other kids join in. "DARE! DARE! DARE!"

A boy with bristly, short-cropped hair pushes his trolley faster and faster, the little wheels rattling and skidding on the concrete, his pumps beating the ground so fast. He scoops his body low, then springs up quick and lands inside the trolley on his knees, holding his hands up high in the air, wiggling his bum and singing, "La la lala, la la lala, la lala, lalalala!" He skitters and bounces along, heading for a huge black shiny car.

"DO IT! DO IT! DO IT!" they all chant.

He grins, his eyes twinkling as he smashes into the side of the car, flying out of the trolley with a triumphant whoop, landing on the ground with a thump. Everyone goes crazy, clapping and whooping, cheering and laughing. He jumps up, dusts himself down and bows.

"Evening entertainment," says Henny, nudging me.

I'm so tired, my arms and legs feel as if they're draining away like bath water. But my mind's buzzing, on hyper alert like a bee. Henny walks over to the smashed car and runs her hand along its graze.

We head off in a huddle of hands and feet and flapping jackets. Boys making rude gestures with their fingers at passing cars, girls rolling their eyes. My arm brushes Henny's as we walk, making a warm loop of something swoop inside me.

"Rule number two," says Henny, sternly, pointing to the cigarettes and drink that some of the others are holding, "don't even think about touching any of that. Out of bounds for you, kitten."

"Don't worry," I say, shrugging her off. "I'm not that stupid. I wouldn't touch that stuff anyway."

Some of the boys kick dead cans along the road, shouting, pushing each other off the kerb, waggling their pink tongues at passersby who keep their eyes down low.

We huddle in a back alley, the noise of the city thundering around us. The girl in the big jumper sits next to me on the kerb. She pulls a thread on her jeans; she licks her finger and rubs at a grey patch on her shoe.

"Hi," she says. "I'm Tia."

"Hello," I say. "D'you know someone called Beckett? He's got brown curly hair. He's nineteen and I really need to find him."

She shakes her head, picks at her fingernails and shrugs.

We sit for ages, just staring into space, with farting and joking from the boys swirling around us like fog. I can't stop thinking about Connor and the little girl and Mum. I can't stop wondering about Beckett. If only I had the photo, maybe someone would recognise him.

"You sure you don't know someone called Beckett?" I yawn. "Really sure?"

Tia shakes her head.

"He's lived here for ages," I say. "You *must* have seen him somewhere."

She laughs, burrowing a finger through a loopy hole in the wool of her jumper.

We wander in our huddle for days, sleeping in the shadows with my heart beating hard on my ribs, invisible to everyone around. Time loops and stretches like Tia's jumper wool, with the days and the night-times fraying and blurring at the seams. Most days I go into the Cathedral and watch the candles flickering and the stained-glass windows reflecting on my hands. Most nights I slide closer to Tia and dream of tall houses with plush carpets and shiny kitchens and cotton-soft beds.

And then one night, the air around us sucks tight.

"Quick," says Henny, tugging Tia and me, pulling us up. "Stay close to me, OK?"

I lug my bag on to my back and run with the rumble of feet through the streets. It's really late; people are everywhere, spilling from pubs with beer breath and loud laughs, running for buses. The thrum of the city pulses in my ears and bangs my body like a drum.

"Where are we going?" I ask Henny.

Henny shrugs. "Dunno."

Round the corner one of the boys starts dancing and whooping, flipping his stringy body around, leaping through the air like lightning. Everyone's clapping and calling out.

"Who's bored?" he taunts, pulling a big metal bar from his bag, waving it in the air, his eyes flashing red with danger. The air crackles with excitement, everyone holding their breath, waiting to see what the boy will do.

He swings the metal bar high and smashes it against a shop front. A huge crack snakes across the window. He bashes it over and over, laughing out loud as a million sparkles of glass scatter at his feet like diamonds. A shrill alarm bell drills through my ears; people scatter like the glass, everything shining with panic.

"Quick," says Henny, yanking on my bag, "go on! Get what you can!"

She pushes me into the deep flood of kids running into the shop. I'm trembling so much; the knot in my tummy is twisting and pulling me back to her, like she's some safe harbour to tie myself on to.

"I can't, Henny," I say. "It's too scary!"

"You have to," she says. "The cops'll be here soon, just get what you can."

I run into the shop, blindly grabbing at the bright sweets and crisps and drinks and shiny magazines that slither and slide in my hands. The boy is a frenzy of smashing, blindly bashing anything in front of him. He grabs a handful of newspapers, scrunches them up, strikes a match and throws it on the paper. Orange flames rise up, licking hungrily, grabbing everything they pass with their long, scorching fingers.

The sound of the nee-nawing police-car sirens comes closer, flashing their lights, turning the whole world blue. And everyone but the boy and me starts running. I stand there, frozen, watching the thick black smoke swirling around me, filling my lungs with fear.

"Quick," calls Henny. "Gabriella, come on!"

My feet won't move. The boy's golden eyes are as wild as the fire.

"I said, come on!" Henny shouts, running in and dragging me out by my sleeve. "You wanna get caught?"

Outside the air is electric, kids scattering like skittles, making faces at the police, running faster than the wind. Henny and me run, our Converse pounding the streets until our feet are stinging and raw. Round the corner and down a back alley, Henny and me climb these cold metal steps that cling to the side of a massive old warehouse. They go on for years, a zigzag of black pencil lines reaching right up to the sky.

"Where are we going, Henny?" I ask.

"Somewhere."

"But where? Where are we?"

"You ask too many questions," Henny snaps. "Just trust me, OK!"

Chapter 11

The top of the metal staircase opens out on to a wide flat roof. Loads of kids are up there already, some of them dancing to loud music that's blaring from some speakers.

"You OK?" asks Tia, sipping Coke from a can.

I nod but inside I'm jittering like mad.

"What did you get?"

I look down at my hands. I feel in my pockets.

"I dropped most of it while I was running," I say, holding out a few chocolate bars and a can of Fanta. "It's really hard with my backpack."

"Share-sies," says Henny, holding her hand out.

I hand her a few bars and snap open the Fanta to share. We stand there looking up at the bright moon hanging over us like a huge white bauble on a Christmas tree.

"Bedtime for you, kitten," she says.

I'm not listening to Henny. She's not the boss of me, but I'm tired so I find a quiet place to wee, then clean my teeth with a minuscule blob of toothpaste and screw the lid back on tight. I make a pillow with my jumper, loop my arm through my backpack straps and lie down. I try to lie still, but I can't stop wriggling around. And every time I let myself drop into that safe black place of sleep my tummy clenches up quick, my eyes flick open wide, and my brain starts buzzing like a bee.

I watch the other kids dancing and everyone sipping and smoking and joking. I think about Grace, all tucked up safe and warm in her bed with the corner of her page turned over and a glass of water on her bedside.

This is my life now.

And it's a thousand years from home.

I watch the dark clouds drifting across the moon and remember when Dad and me watched for the solar eclipse from the window. I keep my eyes on Tia, huddled in the corner, gnawing the sleeve of her too-big jumper and I can't remember what day it is because everything's blurred into one. Is it Sunday tomorrow or Monday? Or Friday?

The flat concrete roof is too hard to get comfy on and although it's still warm from daytime sunshine, cool gusts of air breeze over me like ghosts. I shiver and think of my bed. I dig my hand deep inside my backpack and hold on to Blue Bunny's ear. I stroke its silky softness between my finger and my thumb and see Beckett's name in biro in my mind. Cars and buses screech in the distance, rumbling through the night. Police cars and ambulances and fire engines rip up the sky with their sirens and turn the white moon blue. I wish Tia would come and be near me. I wish someone would hold my hand.

I tear open a KitKat and nibble off the chocolate around the edge. I don't mind about my teeth. They can get all covered in plaque and rot away. See if I care. I munch into the wafer then let it go soggy and melt on my tongue. I jangle the money in my pocket without making a sound.

I think about Dad.

I think about Mum.

I think about that boy Connor and that girl Jayda and think how funny it is that they look like me. I eat a Twix and take another sip of Fanta.

How can I find Beckett? I close my eyes and search inside for a special super power that will miraculously magic him here. I whizz through the tunnels of my veins, in and out of my muscles, all through my body and find the magic tucked deep inside my heart. I concentrate hard so it builds stronger and brighter inside me. I imagine the picture of Beckett and watch it slip and slide through my thoughts, blurring and reshaping through the years until I can see his nineteen-year-old face. He's standing somewhere in Manchester, or sleeping in a bed on a cotton-soft pillow. I send out my silver super-power searchlight and watch it shine from my heart, zooming through the city, in and out of the houses, up and down the roads, searching for him, until the whole of Manchester is shimmering.

My eyes are burning like mad with being awake for so long. I rummage in my bag for my sketchbook and pens and under the light of the bluish moon I draw the huge warehouse building and the boy dancing and the flames licking his shoes. I draw the black metal steps zigzagging up to the clouds. I draw Henny's pink hair. I draw Tia, as small and skinny as a skeleton, and make her jumper even huger so it trails right down to the ground, catching the leaves as she walks. A few other kids give up dancing and huddle in shabby heaps around me, sniffing and scuffling. I make my eyes big to keep them open until they sting like crazy. And when I can't draw or chew or sip or keep them open any longer I close my eyes.

Much later, when the morning sun spills pink on the sky, Henny comes and lies close by me.

"Henny!" I whisper. "Where's the boy?"

She cuddles herself with her long stringy arms and yawns.

"Probably wanted a bed for the night," she whispers. "And a meal. Trouble is, I think he went a bit too far. He might get sent down for arson."

"Henny?" I whisper. "What's arson?"

"Sssshhhhh," she says, touching her finger gently on my lips.

Chapter 12

A while ago

My feet are covered in blisters and my Converse stink. I keep thinking about food, proper food. I'm tired of chocolate. I'd like a big roast dinner or some beans on toast, and a steaming hot bath full of bubbles.

"We could go down my place," says Tia, flapping her jumper sleeves.

"It's her mum's place," Henny explains. "We go there sometimes when she's working."

"Why don't you stay there?" I ask. "Why don't you sleep there?"

Tia wraps her arms around her skinny shoulders and looks the other way.

It's weird being indoors with the front door shut and the clock ticking and the sunshine streaming through the window. We make fat cheese and pickle sandwiches and cups of tea with two sugars each. We attack a packet of HobNobs, snuggle up close on the sofa and dunk them in our tea. We watch *The Jeremy Kyle Show* and *Judge Judy*. Judge Judy is shouting at a woman who's accusing her sister of stealing antiques from their ninety-eight-year-old mum. Henny's rummaging through Tia's mum's stuff, pulling open drawers, reading private letters.

When it's my turn in the bathroom, I sit in the chalky pink bath and hold the shower thing over me for ages, until the room is full of steam and the blue tiles are dripping. I'm as pink and shiny as a piglet. I soap my hair so it's all bubbles on top then watch the foamy grey water rush over my skin and swirl down the drain with a SLLUUURRGE!

We bundle into Tia's bedroom. Henny dries our

hair until it's shiny; we talk about made-up stuff like going on holiday and what we're having for dinner and boyfriends.

"Where you off to this year?" Henny asks, taming my curls with Tia's straighteners so they hang like a heavy brown cloak.

"Italy," I say, remembering the TV programme with the beardy man.

"I'm going to Disneyland," she says. "A whole bunch of us are going for a month."

Tia paints some of her mum's bright pink varnish on our nails and then we do stripes and dots and our fingers look like dolly mixtures. "I'm going somewhere exotic with my boyfriend," she says, "with big white beaches and a pool. We're so in love I think he's going to ask me to marry him. He's got me this huge diamond ring because he earns millions!"

My tummy clenches up. I think of Amy spending all Dad's money. I wonder where they are.

"I like this," says Tia, blowing on her nails, her dull eyes shining.

"I don't understand," I say, sorting out my backpack.

"Why don't you stay here, Tia?"

Tia's eyes grow huge. She presses her lips together, until they're just a thin white line. She shakes her head.

"You have to respect people's privacy, kitten," says Henny. "We all have stuff we don't want to talk about."

We lie on Tia's bed like happy sardines in a tin. Henny tucks one arm under my neck and one under Tia's and squishes us close so our heads almost melt into hers. "My little chicks," she says, planting a kiss on our foreheads.

I rest my head on her arm and close my eyes. The smell of the flowery shampoo wafts up my nose and makes me think about Grace and her mum. I look at Henny and Tia. I listen to our hearts beating, to our gentle breathing, and wish we could stay like this forever.

"You trust me, don't you?" Henny says, leaning up on one elbow and looking at me.

I nod, trying my best to pull away from the heavy sleep monster that's chasing my eyes.

"Why?" asks Tia.

"Nothing," says Henny, stroking my hair. "Just wondering."

I'm fighting to stay awake, but keep tumbling out of dolly mixture heaven into a huge, black, bottomless well.

"Wondering what?" says Tia.

"Oh," says Henny, "it's just Kingdom's on at me again. He has this little job he wants us to do."

Tia turns over and presses her face against the wall.

"You'll help me, kitten?" says Henny, looping both arms around me, like I was a baby, and cuddling me close. "Won't you?"

"Come on," says Tia, jumping up suddenly and jolting me awake. "Time to go."

"Can't we stay longer?" I ask, longing to fold into the covers for the rest of my life.

"No!" she shouts. She shakes her head again. "Come on, we have to leave."

Outside, the sun is sharp on my eyes. We share out a packet of Haribo Tia found in her little brother's bedroom and head for Piccadilly Gardens. A few kids are there, messing about, and we lie in the sun chatting, but Henny keeps checking the time.

"I'm going to spy on my mum's house again," I say.

"See if I can spot Beckett."

"You don't need to worry about them any more," Henny says. "You've got us now. We're family."

I lean in close to her and rest my tired head on her arm. "I just need to," I say. "I like you both, but I need to find Beckett. I need to start asking people if they know where he is."

"You can't ask anyone," says Henny, "because they'll get all suspicious about who you are and then pull you in."

Henny suddenly leaps up like she's been struck by lightning. She races off towards this big black car. A tinted window slides down, a hand comes out, pops some chewing gum in Henny's mouth and her head disappears inside.

"Henny's all right," says Tia, stretching a Haribo until it snaps, "but you can't trust her or anything she says."

I pull out my sketchbook and draw a road full of cars, a Mickey Mouse, a Minnie Mouse, a Donald Duck, and a tree with loads of hearts hanging from the branches like red apples. I look at Tia, pulling threads from her jeans, and sketch her bony cheeks, her dark shadowy eyes, her pointy nose. I draw her wispy hair dancing with the breeze.

"S'good," she says, peering over my shoulder. "Wish I could draw."

When Henny gets back she's all jumpy, her eyes twitching like a rabbit's. Tia makes a huffing sound; she flashes her eyes at me like she's trying to say something and wanders off. And I don't know why, but my tummy starts flipping like a fish struggling for life on the sand.

"Know what I was saying earlier?" Henny says, twiddling my hair through her fingers.

I nod and start sketching her shoes.

Henny's eyes are still twitching like mad. She sits next to me on the grass, knots a skinny arm through mine, and gives me a kiss on the cheek.

"I'm telling the truth when I say we're family," she says. "And family'll do anything for one another, true?"

I nod and swallow hard; Tia's words spin through my mind.

"I just need a bit of help," she says. "Tonight. It won't take long."

"OK," I say, "but if I help you, will you help me find Beckett?"

"Course!" Henny laughs. "Obviously! I promise!"

Chapter 13

"**R**ight!" says Henny. "Ready?"

I stand and face the red brick wall of these luxury apartments, the little bathroom window above me reflecting the light of the moon. I block everything else out and concentrate on Beckett. I have to do this.

"You sure you'll help me afterwards?" I say, a little knot of fear catching in my throat.

Henny nods. She chews on a fingernail. "Course, kitten," she smiles. "Trust me! And remember, as soon as you're in, scoot straight round to the back door and open it. It's all you have to do."

Henny links her fingers together and makes a cradle

for me to rest my foot in. She heaves me up so I'm level with the little window that's resting slightly ajar. I wriggle my finger through the gap and pop the metal arm thing up so the window flies open. I'm trembling inside, my ears are thrumming, my tummy's full of snakes.

"OK?"

I nod. Henny lifts me higher and higher until I can just about squeeze my shoulders through the gap. I scuffle my feet up the wall, and, feeling like Spiderman, I pull my knees up on to the tiles. Careful not to clatter anything I jump down into the bath, climb out and stumble through the dark towards the door. I flick the switch and the bathroom floods with light. It's the hugest I've ever seen, with creamy tiles and soft white towels and these taps, so shiny the light bounces off of them and explodes into stars.

"Hurry!" hisses Henny. "It's really late, they'll be home any minute."

I have to quickly use the toilet and it's hard because Henny keeps hissing from outside the window. As if I'm not freaked out enough as it is, sitting on someone else's toilet in the middle of the night. But I can't help that my tummy's turned to mush. It's her fault for making me do this – not mine!

I don't have time to wash my hands because Henny's having a manic attack outside, but I make sure Blue Bunny's still tucked in my pocket for luck. Then I race through the dark hallway, my heart banging loud as a drum. I stand facing the back door. It has so many locks. I pull up a chair, undo the big brass bolt at the top and twist the grey key thing next to it. Then I undo the bottom bolt and the key next to that, then I'm stuck, staring at the keyhole in the middle that's empty.

"What's happening?" whispers Henny from the other side of the door.

"The middle key's missing!" I hiss. "I can't do it!"

"Look around then," she snaps. "Come on, kitten, use your noddle. People hang them near the door, put them in drawers, on the top ledge. Come on!"

Trembling like a jelly, I climb up and run my fingers along the ledge. "It's not there, Henny!" I say.

"Then look around!" she says.

I check around the doorframe and scuffle through

the things in the kitchen drawer, my hands dripping with sweat. I need the toilet again. I can't breathe. I hunt around the curly brass hooks with mugs swinging from them and in the big flowery bowl full of fruit.

"If there's a mat by the door," Henny hisses, through the bubbly glass window, "look under it!"

I lift up the mat and the big brass key glints at me like treasure. I fumble to get it in the lock, my heart racing faster than dogs. When Henny bursts through the door I can't stop my tears from spilling over.

"We haven't got time for tears," she says. "We have to be quick!"

I sniff them back. I hold on to Blue Bunny's ear. I stroke Beckett's name.

"Look," she says, "you did good. Now wait here, OK? And shout if anyone comes!"

I wait on the step, listening hard for cars and watching out for headlights while Henny darts through the apartment gathering things and then running back and stuffing them in my rucksack. I'm jittering so much I don't think I can stand up any more. I'm scared I might wet myself. Henny's already got two laptops and an iPod and handfuls of jewellery. She grabs some credit cards from a drawer and three passports and loads of important-looking papers.

"Why d'you need those, Henny?" I whisper.

She looks at me with these cold hard eyes I've never seen before.

"Don't ask," she snaps, "just do as I say!"

I nod, a huge balloon of fear swelling in my throat.

"Right," she says. "Now we have to do the whole thing in reverse, OK? You have to lock the door, put the mat straight with the key under it and climb back out of the bathroom window."

I want to run, to fly far away from here on black tattooed angel wings. Grace's mum's shed flashes in my eyes, her roses round the door, Kitty's soft fur nuzzling me. But the volcano is coming towards me with its hot lava splashing in Henny's cold eyes.

Quivering so much my teeth are clattering in my head, I shut the door. I twist the big brass key and slip it back under the mat. I do the bottom locks up and I'm just about finishing the top ones when Henny bangs on the door.

"Quick!" she hisses. "They're back!"

Like the wind whipping litter through the air I shove the chair back in place and snap the lights off. I grab two bananas from the flowery bowl and make a race for the bathroom. I close the toilet seat down and I'm just about to climb in the bath and struggle for the window when I hear the front door bang shut.

I freeze, cold and hot flushing in my cheeks, ice and fire, running down my legs. My heart stops beating. My ears are throbbing with blood.

"Come on, kitten!" whispers Henny. "Climb out!"

I pull myself up on the window ledge, sending a shampoo bottle skittering across the tiles.

"Sshhhhhh!" hisses Henny! "Just hurry, will you! Jump!"

I squeeze my shoulders out of the window. I wriggle the rest of my body through and fall with a heavy thud, twisting my ankle when I hit the ground. Henny grabs me and shoves us both in a bush, slinging her arm round my neck, pressing her hand over my mouth so the pulse in her fingers beats fast on my lips. The lights in the apartment flash on and flood the garden with light. It's not soft, warm, honey light though; it's sharper than icicles and stabs at my eyes. I think I might explode. Everything is jangling inside me.

A man opens the bathroom window and pokes his head out into the night.

"See anything, darling?" a woman's voice trills.

Henny and me are so quiet even the breeze stops moving through the trees. We hold our breath. Henny's grip gets tighter on my mouth. The man's head darts backwards and forwards, owl eyes shining in the dark.

"Anybody out there?" he booms.

He waits, listening, watching for the bushes to move.

"Oh, come on, darling," the woman says. "Let's go to bed. It must've been the breeze."

When the window clicks shut we stay stiller than statues, until every light is out and the garden is plunged into darkness.

"Quick!" says Henny, jumping up. "We're late!"

"Late for what?" I say stumbling up the path. But Henny ignores me. She grabs my sleeve and marches me up the road.

"Wait there!" she says, shoving me behind a skip.

"And don't keep asking questions."

I shrink behind the yellow skip and lick a graze on my hand. My ankle is throbbing like mad. I pull Blue Bunny out of my pocket and snuggle into his ear while I watch Henny lean through the window of the big black car. She pulls the stolen stuff out of my bag, hands it over and comes back smiling, popping a big pink bubblegum balloon in my face.

"Come on," she smiles, snaking her arm through mine. "You did good tonight, kitten. Real good!"

We walk for ages, avoiding the CCTV cameras and the loud people spilling out of the clubs, me hobbling on my poorly ankle. I ache for my bed, for Dad, for home.

"I can't walk any further, Henny," I say, tears welling up and stinging my eyes. "My ankle hurts too much. I think I might've broken it!"

Henny laughs. "Oh, poor kitten," she says, stroking my hair. "Hang on for a little bit longer then I promise I'll take a look at it."

"What if it's broken?" I say. "How do we get to the hospital?"

"We can't go to the hospital, Gabriella," she says, gently squeezing my hand. "It's too risky. But I'll look after you, trust me."

We walk for maybe ten minutes more or an hour or a day, I'm not sure. Time in Manchester is stretching and shrinking like gum, blurring and sliding. My ankle is a hot sharp furnace of pain, waving its arms for attention. And when I can't walk any more, Henny hides me behind some bins down an alleyway.

"Stay there," she says, giving my ankle a quick rub, "and don't move. If someone from a club comes and pees against the wall turn your face away and keep very still. OK? Hungry?"

I nod, but my nod is a lie.

I feel sick. Sick with worry, sick with pain, sick with fear.

I'm sick of everything twisting and turning inside me. I pull up the leg of my jeans and touch my fingers on my big red apple ankle that's throbbing and shining in the dark. I need Beckett. I need someone bigger. I'm tired of keeping on moving.

*

When Henny arrives back she has a mountain of burgers and chips and two massive Cokes in her hands.

"How did you get it?" I say, slurping on a Coke.

She taps her finger on her nose. "Don't be nosy," she says, grinning.

Henny pulls me up and I limp through a long maze of alleyways, until we find a quiet shop doorway to sleep in. It smells of old men's wee and smoke, but we huddle up close.

I stare into space, nibbling my chips, swallowing my burger. It sits in my stomach like a cold, hard fist.

Chapter 14

When the day pours pale steely grey paint over the night and the city wakes for breakfast I scribble a quick note for Henny and slip away. My ankle is stiff and pounding, still shiny apple red and sore. I hobble along fast towards Mum's.

Rumbling thunder fills the clouds, stretching them tight like fat grey water balloons ready to burst on my head. I stop for a while to rest and draw the huge grumbling clouds inside a giant's tummy, with hundreds of stick people running for shelter. I give them tiny umbrellas and draw minuscule drops of rain lashing down. I think about Mrs Evans and wonder what art project they're working on now. I draw a big, wooden ark and an old man Noah in a cloak with a long curly beard and great waves crashing and swirling around him.

I clink the coins in my pocket and duck into the bakers to buy a warm bread roll. I head to Mum's and hide behind the fence and the bins, nibbling while I wait. I watch the dust sweep up the road and yesterday's washing tug at clothes pegs like headless people straining to run.

When the big hairy man comes out of Mum's house I freeze. He hops on his motorbike, clips up his helmet and roars away, making the ground underneath me shake. That boy Connor presses his face on the window, squishing his lips and nose, waving goodbye to his dad. I see Mum grab his arm and yank him away. Connor shouts. Mum slaps. I rub my ankle. I fidget in my pocket for Blue Bunny.

School kids in purple jumpers, swinging yellow book bags from their fists, and mums pushing babies in buggies, spill out of the houses like popcorn. I think of that song, *The wheels on the bus go round and round.*

The Mummies on the bus go chatter, chatter, chatter. The children on the bus go play, play, play.

I roll my arms round and round like me and Grace used to do and silently mouth out the words. When Mum steps out of the door with Jayda in the pushchair and Connor trailing behind I shrink back. My heart clatters like mad; so loud I'm scared she'll hear it.

"The problem with football," says Connor, stopping to do up his shoelace, "is you have to kick the ball really, really hard to get it in the goal. My friend Musti can do it, but I never can."

Mum grabs his hand and clamps it round the blue handle of the pushchair. She looks up at the thunderclouds and frowns. "That's probably, Connor Marshall, because you take after your stupid, useless dad," she snaps. "Now stop rabbiting and hurry up."

When they're out of view and the street has emptied I dash across the road. I peep through the front window, rubbing the glass clean with my palm to get a better look. My tummy swishes like seawater. Toys litter the floor; mountains of bags and clothes avalanche off the sofa. Two green plastic breakfast bowls and spoons by the telly sit in spilt milk puddles. It's weird, Mum living here and me never having been inside. I press my nose and lips where Connor pressed his and when I'm certain no one's watching, I take a big deep breath and knock on the door. I wait for ages, twiddling Blue Bunny's ear, sending out my special silver searchlight to Beckett.

I wait for ages, knocking again and again, wishing that I'd hear Beckett thunder down the stairs to open up the door. But when I've waited forever and he doesn't come I go back to the baker lady and buy Henny a lovely warm bread roll. Then I race to find her as fast as my ankle will let me.

"You should just forget about him," she says, tearing chunks of bread off and rolling squidgy dough balls between her palms. "I told you, you don't need him or anyone else. You've got me now!"

"I like you, Henny," I say, sliding towards her. "But I do need to find Beckett. Then we can all be a family together. You'll really like him too."

"It's useless," she says. "You don't even know if he lives in Manchester any more. He might even be dead! You said that Connor boy had never even heard of him."

A tight ball of panic knots in my throat. "Don't say that," I say. "Don't say he's dead, Henny, please!"

Henny licks the crumbs off her bright pink fingernails and looks like she's eating sweets.

"He might not even be that nice any more," she says. "You haven't seen him for years. People change. Just saying."

"But you said you'd help!" I say. "You promised, Henny! You said if I helped you then you'd help me. You said it's what families do."

I stare at her, my body filling with panic.

"Oh, don't be boring, kitten," she says, jumping up. "We *are* family and we *do* do stuff for each other. I'm looking after you, aren't I? You just got me breakfast. That's being family, that's *doing* stuff."

"We could ask people?" I say. "Or make signs and put them up and hope Beckett sees them? There's probably loads of stuff we could be doing, Henny, but I can't do it on my own. I need your help. *Please?*"

Henny rolls her eyes. "It's not the end of the world or anything," she says. "Come on; let's have some fun today."

I follow her all the way back to Piccadilly Gardens, limping and sulking.

I don't want to be with Henny any more. I just want Beckett.

But it's hard to leave her.

"Stay here," she says, when we catch up with the other kids. "And don't move, OK?"

I sit on the grass and watch her linger on the kerb, smiling, twirling her stripy hair round her finger. A man with a shiny bald head strolls up to Henny, she loops her arm through his and they walk away, chattering and laughing. Tia plops down on the grass next to me and wraps her arms around her knees.

"You OK, Gabriella?" she asks.

I nod, feeling for Blue Bunny in my pocket.

"Did she make you do stuff?"

My eyes twitch. I shake my head. "Nothing much," I lie, pulling my sock up over my ankle.

"You don't always have to do what she says," says Tia. "She's not the boss of you."

When Henny comes back her eyes are shining, her cheeks flushed pink. "Result!" she says, pulling me up and flashing money in my face.

"Is that Kingdom?" I ask, remembering the name Henny said at Tia's.

"No!" she says. "Kingdom never gets out of his car!"

"Who was it then?"

"No one special," she says, smiling. She turns to Tia. "Wanna come with us?" she says. "I've promised kitten some fun."

Tia flaps her sleeves, looks up at the huge, dark clouds threatening to tip rain on our heads, and nods.

First we wander down the street, window-shopping, imagining all the things we'd buy if we won the lottery. Then we trail through the shops trying on loads of cool stuff, giggling and laughing so much I almost forget about my ankle.

Henny dares us to go into this big department store and pretend we're on that programme *Don't Tell The Bride*, buying bridesmaid stuff. I think about Dad all trussed up like a turkey in his grey suit and pink shirt. I think about Amy and her two dresses and all the money. I wonder where they are now and wish I had a charger for my phone. But you can't say no to

Henny. She doesn't really allow it and when we're in the shop she acts so grown-up, bossing the assistant around while we try on all these really expensive dresses and shoes and put sparkly tiaras on our heads that I almost believe it's true. I almost believe that we really are going to be on the telly.

Tia and me practise walking up the aisle, all slow-mo and serious, while Henny talks to the lady about what flowers would go best with our clothes. I only want roses, white ones, like the ones around Grace's mum's door, but the lady's saying tulips are in fashion. I wonder if Amy and Dad had roses or tulips at their wedding. I bet Amy had a mega-sparkly tiara.

If Amy would've let me be a bridesmaid I know what dress I'd choose. It's not a silky one or a puffy one. It's not even the most expensive. It's one tucked at the end of the rail made of white cotton with sparkles on like the kind of thing Laura from *Little House on the Prairie* might wear. I wouldn't have spoilt it for Amy. I would have even worn whatever dress she chose. Just so I could be there with Dad.

When we pretend we're on *My Big Fat Gypsy Wedding,*

we get totally hysterical. Tia's giggles fire out like a machine gun; she doubles over, clutching her tummy, tears squeezing from the corners of her eyes. Henny's voice gets louder and louder, demanding puffier dresses for us with loads more frills. Then she trips over. The silver high-heeled shoes she's wearing jab the corner of the silky blue dress she's yanked on over her leggings and top, and the loudest ripping sound ever splits the air in half.

For a moment she rolls on the floor, laughing, her arms and legs waggling about like a beetle on its back. Then she lies very still trying to melt into the carpet pattern, smothering her giggles, hoping the assistant lady didn't hear. But the lady's ears prick up, she struts over to us with her arms crossed and a sour lemon look fixed on her face. She takes a sharp breath in.

Tia and me panic. We frantically start pulling off our dresses, throwing our own clothes on, and grabbing hold of our bags. The assistant slams her hand on the desk, pursing her lips so they look like a hamster's bottom.

"I think we've had *quite* enough of this!" she snaps.

"And I do hope you realise that *all* damages must be paid for!"

Henny freezes for less than a second, her eyes flashing, her brain cogs turning. "Run!" she shouts, scrambling out of the dress. "Follow me!"

Henny, Tia and me run faster than the wind, our hair flying out like kite strings behind us. We push through the shoppers, out of the Wedding department, through Children's. We fly down the escalator, past Make-Up and on to the street outside.

"Stop there!" shouts a red-faced man in a navy blue jumper with *Security* embroidered on it. He pulls out a radio thing and shouts, "Kids," and chases us, thrashing his hands about in the air.

But my eyes are on Henny; I'm running behind her, my ankle throbbing, my backpack digging into my shoulder.

"Do you hear me?" shouts the security man, panting behind us. "I said, Stop! Right! There!"

"Quick!" says Henny, grabbing our hands and weaving us through the swarms of shoppers, darting into an alleyway, pushing us through a little doorway and up some red metal stairs. The man keeps shouting, his voice echoing in my ears.

We huddle in a boiler room full of hissing and clunking and sit on the floor to catch our breath. Henny and Tia are laughing so much I think they might wet themselves. My tummy's twisting, my heart's clattering, everything's jangling inside. And I'm just about to check my ankle when something tugs at my hair.

"No!" I say, freeing a glittering tiara from my tangles. Guilty feelings tumble through me; my eyes fill up with tears. "I've still got it on! I've stolen a tiara!"

Chapter 15

The thunder growls and the black clouds throw bucketfuls of raindrops, scattering everyone like marbles.

"C'mon," says Henny, tipping her head up and catching the rain in her mouth. "I've got an idea."

"I'm going home," says Tia. "I'm not hanging out in this."

She tugs my arm. "I could probably sneak you in tonight," she whispers. "If you want?"

"I thought you never stayed there?"

She lifts her shoulders up to her ears and they drop back down like a heavy sack of potatoes. Henny crosses her arms in front of her chest. She makes this big sulky face, sighs and turns her back on Tia.

"Go with her if you want," she huffs, glaring at me. "Miss out on all the fun I've got planned. See if I care!"

My tummy starts twisting. I look at Tia. I look at Henny's back all hunched up and angry. "Can Henny come too?" I ask.

Tia stretches a jumper sleeve until it's extra long and wraps it round her hand like a bandage. She shakes her head. "Too many people," she says. "My dad'll hear. He hears everything."

Henny flies round, stabbing Tia with her glassy eyes. "Don't fret yourself, Tia," she hisses. "I wouldn't wanna stay at your place anyway. Full of pervs."

Tia touches my arm. "I'll look out for you," she whispers, catching the rain in her palm and turning to go.

I don't want to go and have fun with Henny and I don't want to go to Tia's. I don't want anything except Beckett, but no one will help. How do you even begin to find someone in a city as big as Manchester?

"Come on!" says Henny, grabbing my hand. "Let's go and see a film."

When we get to the cinema, Henny goes mad buying stuff with the cash she got from that man. We get two super-sized Cokes, two boxes of popcorn, a packet of Minstrels and a packet of jelly babies to share. While we're standing in the bustle of people she winks at me then slips her hand in a lady's bag, pulling out a purse and a mobile phone. I glare at her and shake my head. She taps her finger on my lips and smiles.

"Right," she whispers, pointing to a crowd of people lining up to give their tickets to the girl. "You just have to look like you're with them, like someone else has your ticket. Stay close and smile. I'll meet you in screen four. OK?"

I freeze. I think about the fish and chips on my very first night with Henny and breaking into that apartment. I think about the stolen tiara that's burning a huge guilty hole in my bag. I'm not the person I was any more. I don't think even Grace would recognise me if she were here.

I shake my head.

"It's just for fun!" she whispers. "It's a buzz!"

"I'm not sure," I say, watching the crowd of people

slowly trailing in.

"We're going to miss it if we don't hurry," she says. "Look, I promise, promise, promise, after the films we'll set about finding Beckett. We won't stop searching until we find him."

I look in her eyes, searching to see if she's telling the truth. "Promise?"

"Promise," she whispers, "we'll look everywhere, we'll search the entire world for him, we'll ask everyone. I promise you we'll find him. Now go on in before it's too late!"

I press myself close to the crowd of people handing tickets over to the girl collecting them. I look at Henny. She winks back. I keep the picture of Beckett's face in my mind, sending my special searchlight shimmering through Manchester. Soon. Soon, I'll find him. Soon he'll tell me what to do. I draw a smile on my face. I nibble on popcorn. I try to look like I'm having a nice time, like I know what everyone's talking about, like I know who everyone is. But my cheeks are scorching; my heart's fluttering like the wings of a butterfly trapped in a net.

"Ticket?" says the girl.

I ignore her, keeping my face down; hiding in the trail of strong perfume the lady in a green, flowery dress is leaving behind her. I edge closer, looking like I'm with her, wishing somehow I were.

"'Ere, you!" says the girl, pinning me to the spot with her stare. "I said, ticket!" She holds her hand out, waiting.

The crowd stops snaking along, suspicious eyes buzz over me like wasps.

"I errm," I say, spinning round, searching for Henny. "I…"

A voice shouts loud in my head. *Run, Gabriella, run!*

I drop my Coke and popcorn and push through the crowd, searching for Henny, my bag thrashing about on my back; my ankle shooting scorching darts of pain up my leg.

"Oy!" shouts a security guard, racing after me. "Come back here!"

Outside, Henny's nowhere to be seen. I run and run and run, avoiding the puddles. I run and run and run, trying to run out of my skin, trying to get away from my life.

Please, Beckett, where are you? I need you so much!

I don't even know where to start looking. I don't even know who to ask.

When I'm far away from the cinema I stop running and check my ankle. I need a bandage. I need to wash my feet.

I open my backpack. It's too heavy. I can't carry it any longer.

So I rummage through the tangle of sleeves and stinky socks and scrunched-up rainbow snips of paper and sweet wrappers. I drag out a bundle of soft cotton clothes stubbled with sharp gritty bits and sift through it all, sorting, wondering what to keep. I drop half my life in the plastic bin and fold the rest up neatly and put it back in my bag.

I pull my phone out of the side pocket.

I press the dead buttons five times, imagining Dad's voice at the other end. Then I kiss the little screen and throw it in the bin.

I start walking and I think about Mum. I imagine knocking at her door and her scooping me in her arms, stroking my wet rat-tail hair, kissing my ankle better, telling me it's all going to be OK. But imagining hurts too much. It makes the tears cram up in my eyes, stinging. Something inside me feels so broken I'm scared it'll never be fixed.

There's only one place left for me to go to. I don't have any choice.

I walk on the pavement, avoiding the cracks, counting from nought to a hundred and back again. I say that war poem in my head, which makes me feel too sad, so I do my seven times table ten times over to help me forget. I go into the bakers and spend the last bit of my money on doughnuts.

"Hello!" says Connor, scooting up to find me behind the bin. "You watching us again?"

I press my finger to his lips. "Shhhh," I say, grabbing his green sweatshirt sleeve and pulling him close. "D'you like doughnuts, Connor?"

He licks his lips, looks over to the house with big owl eyes and nods.

"D'you have to stay here?" I say. "Or are you allowed to the swings?"

"I'll go ask," he says, scooting in circles across the road.

"Don't tell on me though," I whisper. "Promise?"

He grins, holds his thumb up, scoots through the front door, shouts to Mum and scoots back out. Jayda appears at the window, following raindrops with her little pink fingertip, making misty kisses on the glass.

The swings are empty. We climb up and hide under the little red-tiled roof bit at the top of the slide, Connor's scooter clanking on the metal. He rubs his tummy. He licks his lips.

"What are prehistoric monsters called when they sleep?" he says.

"Errrm, I don't know. What are prehistoric monsters called when they sleep?"

"Dinosnores! Silly!" he laughs.

I look at Connor with blank eyes, the broken bit clanging inside me, making it too hard to concentrate on his words.

"OK, then," he chuckles, rolling his eyes upwards, searching in his joke bank for another. "Why didn't the banana snore?"

"I don't know," I say, digging my hand in the doughnut bag. "Why didn't the banana snore?"

"Because he didn't want to wake up the rest of the bunch!"

I make a pretend laugh and Connor's eyes shine.

"Connor?" I say carefully, handing him a doughnut. "You sure you don't know someone called Beckett?"

He draws his knees up to his chin and wraps his arms around them like a bow on a parcel. He shakes his head.

"Not even if you try to remember really hard?" I say.

"I told you," he says. "I've never heard of him. Not ever."

But something in his voice tells me he's lying. So I try a different way.

"Have you ever heard Mum, I mean, have you ever heard *your* mum talking about him?"

He shakes his head, fidgets himself away from me. He sinks his teeth into the doughnut and lets the jam trickle down his chin like blood. We sit in silence for ages, watching the rain drip from the little red roof, pressing our lips in the sugar so they sparkle like snow.

"You know that bunny you've got?" I say eventually.

"That yellow one, the one you were holding before?"

Connor keeps his eyes down low. He pokes his shiny tongue out and licks the sugar off his lips.

"Well," I say. "Who gave it to you?"

He twitches, shutting his face like a book, shrinking away from me.

Chapter 16

That does it. I can't help snapping.

"It's really important you tell me, Connor!" I say. "I think Beckett gave you the bunny and I need to find him. *Urgently!*"

"Stop asking me questions," Connor yells. "I told you! I don't know him. I've never heard of him!"

"Does a man with brown curly hair ever come over?" I ask. "He looks a bit like me. A bit like you, Connor! You must have seen him. Your mum *must've* mentioned him."

"My dad's got curly hair."

"Yes, but I don't mean your dad," I say. "I mean

someone younger than your dad, but older than me. I wish I had his photo. Think hard, Connor, it's really, really important."

He suddenly stands up and makes a leap for a red metal pole.

"I'm not allowed to say," he blurts out, his hands squeaking on the wet metal. "I promised."

My heart bangs on my ribs, my tummy twists in a knot.

"So you do know him then?" I ask. "You know who Beckett is?"

Connor swings his legs high. He jumps back on to the platform and stretches out, tummy down, in the wet.

"I told you, I'm not allowed to say," he says, launching his scooter clattering down the slide. He follows it headfirst landing in a heap at the bottom.

"Don't go, Connor!" I say, panicking.

He stares up at me through the raindrops dripping from his eyelashes. Just crumpled there he looks so small.

"Does she hit you?" I ask in a tiny voice.

A shadow falls across Connor's face. Then he scrabbles himself up, hops on his scooter and scoots away.

"Come back," I say, whizzing down the slide, running to catch him up. "Please, Connor! Please tell me! I need to know!"

He skids to a halt, scuffing the toe of his trainer along the ground, spinning round to face me. "I'm not allowed to say!"

"Not allowed to say what, Connor, not allowed to say what?"

"I'm not allowed to say anything!" he shouts, punching my face with his words, scooting away from me fast. He shouts over his shoulder, "No one must know! He's dead, Connor, remember, he's dead, he's dead!"

I climb on a swing and pump my legs so fast I can see the wet rooftops shining over the fence. My brain is whizzing at a hundred miles an hour. A lump as big as a hard-boiled egg has swelled up in my throat. Beckett's not dead! He can't be! I'd know if he'd died. Mum would've called Dad, she would!

I swing higher and higher, the rain splashing my

cheeks, the wind whipping my hair in my face. I leap off and land on the ground with a thud, a dart of red-hot pain firing from my ankle up my leg.

I need to think. I pick up my bag and start walking. I dig in my pocket for Blue Bunny's ear, scuffling my fist in the soft empty space. My heart clatters like mad.

I drop to the ground and tear open my bag, pulling out the neat pile of stuff, searching for Blue Bunny. I'm not a baby. I just need him.

I turn it all upside down, a kaleidoscope of coloured pens rolling away, my clothes soaking up the puddles like sponges. *Blue Bunny, where are you?*

I check in the side pockets. I hold the empty bag upside down and shake. I peer inside, hoping like a birthday party magician, he'll appear. Then I stuff everything I own back in the bag and, avoiding the cracks, retrace my steps to the bin.

He'll be in the bin; I know it. He'll be all droopy and wet from the rain, sad and angry at being left alone. I fill myself up with my special silver searchlight power and send it shimmering ahead of me to let Blue Bunny know I'm on my way.

On top of all my discarded stuff are loads of soggy chips and half-eaten burgers. I dip my hands in and scuffle through the rubbish trying not to get ketchup slime on my fingers. Please, Blue Bunny, *Please!*

I dig right in, my heart thumping, picking out my books and scraps, my throat closing up and gagging at the rubbishy stink.

He is here; I know it.

I can feel it in my bones; I can feel him getting closer.

I look up through the grey thundery clouds searching for God and I send him a little wave. I feel around in my pocket again just to make sure, one last time that Blue Bunny's not there.

I blink away the tears pinching my eyes. I look around to make sure no one's watching and start pulling everything in the bin on to the pavement. I don't care if I make a mess. I just need to find him. I sink my arms, elbow deep, into the rubbish, rain dribbling down the back of my neck, melting the bits of scattered paper to mush. The stolen tiara winks at me, spinning my tummy into panic. But I don't want that! I don't care about tiaras. I just want Blue Bunny!

"You all right, pet?" asks a lady walking by with a little brown dog, straining on his lead.

I keep my eyes on the pile of rubbish, quickly covering the glinting tiara with the scraps. I want to say, *I didn't steal it, I've never stolen a thing in my life before Manchester, it's just...*

Her kind face reminds me of the cupcake lady in the park, and makes a waterfall gush through me, almost spilling me over the edge.

I shrug my shoulders. I shake my head. "M'OK."

Her little brown dog stops. He sniffs the burger. He licks the ketchup and tugs away the meat. I smile and pat his head. I wish I could bundle him on my lap and hold him there forever. Then he lifts his leg to wee and the hot yellow stream splashes my jeans and runs through the rubbish like a river.

"Ooops! Sorry, pet," laughs the lady, snapping at the dog's lead and pulling him away. "You cheeky thing, Bruno! What to do with you, eh?"

I try to find a little smile to plug up my tears because it is kind of funny what the dog did. It's the kind of thing people video and send in to one of those telly programmes. But I can't find a smile anywhere. And the pee bleeds through my jeans and makes me think about all the germs touching my skin. I can't stop the tears from shuddering out, shaking my shoulders, stinging my eyes, salting my lips. I peer into the bottom of the bin at the thick layer of black sticky gunge, hoping to see two bright bunny eyes peering up at me.

I shove the rubbish back in the bin and throw more of my own stuff away too. I'm tired of my heavy bag. I stoop down, resting my back against the hard, damp wall, balancing my sketchbook on my lap, and draw a beautiful rainbow arching up over a really pretty house with white roses round the door. I draw a Beckett-like man, and a girl and a white pony with soft brown eyes, and a bright red scooter. For a moment my picture looks perfect and I'd like to show it to Mrs Evans. Then a big raindrop sploshes from the gutter and smudges the colours so it looks like it's crying.

I wonder about Beckett being dead, about Blue Bunny being lost. I wonder about Dad and Amy getting married and Connor and Mum and that toddler girl, Jayda. I think about everything horrid and sad in my life and it all starts building up inside like this huge vat of volcano lava gushing towards me, threatening to swallow me whole.

Then this cool minty feeling sweeps over me. It's like when you have a filling in your tooth and the dentist gives you an injection and then drills a hole so big all the nerve endings in your teeth are raw and waving to the world. But because of the injection you can't feel one tiny thing. And he's talking about what you like to do at school and you're there with your mouth open wide, dribbling. And you're watching the little mobile of butterflies swinging in the breeze, not feeling the sharp bits of tooth swilling about in your mouth.

Suddenly, I don't even care about the dog wee touching my skin. I imagine Beckett dead, dead, dead under the dark, wormy earth. I imagine Blue Bunny munched up by the bin men. I imagine Dad spending all the money, Amy laughing at me. I remember Mum hitting me and imagine Connor telling on me. I think about that girl Jayda and her chunky little leg waiting for Mum's big, hard hand.

I stop caring about the CCTV cameras, about my

tummy rumbling like mad, about my ankle throbbing.

I stop caring for anything.

At all.

Chapter 17

I walk in the grey rain for years, getting soaked right through to my skin. I sit in a shop doorway and watch everyone's feet slap the wet ground. They pass by without noticing me. All walking to somewhere dry. I wander through the dripping maze of streets, feeling invisible, looking for the angel-tattoo lemon man and the silver statue people.

But everyone's run for cover.

Everyone's gone home.

When it's late and I can't walk any more I tuck myself behind a skip in an alleyway and make myself a home from a soggy cardboard box. I try drawing roses on it, making them climb up the sides. But my pens don't work so well because everything's too wet.

I don't let myself think about anything. Especially not Beckett. Instead I let the cool minty feeling sweep over me and numb it all away. All the next day no one notices me. No one smiles or catches my eye. I'm a half-dead ghost pacing the streets with aching bones, looking for somewhere comfy to rest.

In the evening, I shelter in the Cathedral doorway and listen to the voices of the choirgirls and boys flying up to the sky like doves. I'd like to go in and sing with them in their special clean, dry choirgirl clothes. I open my mouth wide and wish a beautiful sound could fly out of me.

"Hey, kitten," says Henny, coming towards me. She leans against the big wooden door and rolls her eyes up at the singing.

"I like it," I say. "They sound like angels."

Henny laughs. She folds her arms in front of her chest and makes a big pink bubble with her gum. "D'you believe in God and all that stuff?" she asks.

I shake my head. "Don't think so, I'm not really sure."

"If he was true," says Henny, "then why is life so crap?"

"Maybe he has too many prayers to answer," I say. "Maybe there's just too many people. Maybe the prayers are all lining up in a queue, waiting for their turn, like people in the supermarket."

I think about Grace and all the tasty things her mum gets from that counter. The things she spreads out on the table for us to pick at. Like salami and special cheese, and those little chicken things on sticks that you dip in peanut sauce.

"Where did you go?" I ask.

Henny tears a loose thread of skin from her thumb and a little trail of blood leaks out. She licks it away with her tongue. "Around," she says.

"But you left me," I say, "at the cinema. They started chasing me and I couldn't find you anywhere. I might've got caught."

Henny shrugs.

"What about Beckett?" I ask. "You promised you'd help me find him. I saw that boy again, my little brother, Connor. He said B... B... Beckett was dead. What do you think, Henny? I think I'd know it if he was. I think I'd feel it inside."

"I think your little brother's talking sense," she says.

"Have you got family?" I ask.

She shakes her head and presses her lips together so they make a thin white line.

"You're my family now," she says. "Me and you, kitten."

"Yes, but we can't keep getting into trouble, can we?" I say. "And we can't just hang around here forever. We need to do something."

"Do what?" she says. "There's nothing to do."

We stand there, sheltering from the rain, listening to the singing, until the choir file out and the vicar man snaps off the lights.

"Let's go," says Henny, dragging me by the sleeve. "There's this little job we need to do for you know who."

I pull away and shake my head, searching in my pocket, wishing Blue Bunny would appear. "No," I say, "I'm not coming. I'm tired, Henny, my ankle's killing me, and I can't keep running."

She pulls a bar of chocolate from her bag and opens

the golden wrapper. She breaks off a chunk, pops it in my mouth and my tummy growls. I haven't eaten for years.

"Come on, it won't take a minute," she smiles, snapping off another chunk.

I stand firm. "I'm not doing that stuff any more, Henny," I say. "I can't. It's too scary. I don't like it."

Then she turns on me, her brown eyes pleading. "Just one last time, kitten," she says. "*Please!*"

The panic in her face burns my heart. But then the minty feeling washes over me, numbing everything out.

"I'm sorry, Henny," I say. "I can't."

Henny's face twists up, making her look ugly. She bites a nail; she hugs herself with her arms. I shake my head and turn to go.

"Don't leave me on my own, kitten," she says. "*Please?*"

"Look, I'll come back for you," I say. "I promise. Once I've found Beckett I'll come and find you. He'll know what to do. It'll all be OK."

Henny slides her back down the huge door until she's sitting on the cold hard stone with her arms wrapped tightly round her knees. A single tear rolls down her cheek. She wipes it away with her sleeve and I wish I could run over and make her better.

"Come with me, Henny!" I say. "We'll hide somewhere until we find Beckett. Somewhere safe, far away from Kingdom."

She tucks her head under her arms, her shoulders shaking with tears. I run over and put my arm around her. I kiss the top of her head. She holds on to my hand, squeezing so hard, like if she lets go she'll slide off the edge of a cliff.

She sniffs and wipes her nose on her sleeve. She looks up at me, mascara smudged down her face. "S'OK," she laughs. "You go, kitten. I'll be all right. You go and find Beckett. But come back for me when you've found him, yeah?"

I nod. I squeeze her shoulders, kiss her again and run away faster than the wind.

The elastic band pulls me to Tia's, but once I'm there I feel weird.

I feel stupid. I don't even know if she's still there, if she'll let me in. I don't know if she'll want me. Her road is empty except for a man walking his dog, his shoulders hunched against the rain, the dog sniffing the puddles. I tuck myself behind a big bush outside her house and sit there for years, yawning. The lights in the flats blink at me, the rain twinkles like glitter, and I wonder if she'll ever look out.

"Quick," Tia whispers, peeping her nose out of her door.

I untangle myself from the bush and splash through the puddles that shine like mirrors in the road. Tia bundles me into her room. She flaps her arms around, shushing me, pressing her finger on my lips, mouthing for me to stay quiet as a mouse. She pulls a wet rat-tail of hair from my cheek, holds it up high and drops it down, smothering a giggle. She twists my jacket sleeve like a dishcloth, making a big grey puddle on the floor. Then she mimes for me to take off my clothes.

Tia hands me a thin yellow towel and pulls some clean, dry clothes from a drawer. We lie on her bed in silence, looking up at the cracks on the ceiling, feeling the sounds from the telly in the next room vibrating against the wall. My fingers slide across the bed, finding

Tia's, and we plait them together like hair.

When the place goes quiet and she's sure everyone's sleeping, Tia creeps into the kitchen to get some food.

I lie on her bed with the minty numbness washing over me, thinking about that pink bath of hers and the hot water and the fruity shampoo. I close my eyes and imagine I'm back at home, with Dad in the next room sipping beers, with me making pictures of cosy houses from scraps.

Then a cold dark shadow falls on my face.

I think it's Dad coming in to say goodnight, but when I flick my eyes open my heart stops beating.

"What the blinking hell have we got here?" says a deep, gruff voice.

This huge, hairy man wearing nothing but boxer shorts, with tattoos all over his arms, is leaning over me. Tia appears at the door, twitching nervously, panic lights flashing in her eyes.

"Tia!" the man hollers, turning to face her. "If you think you can smuggle your street trash into this house you've got another think coming! D'you hear me?"

Tia shrinks back against the wall, trembling as his

huge tattooed hands grab my arm and yank me off the bed. He closes his fat fingers around my waist, picks me up like an insect, opens the front door and throws me back outside in the rain.

"And don't even think about coming back!" he growls, as I land on the ground with a thud. "Do you hear me?"

And it's not until I've run faster than the speed of light, away from Tia's, and back to the Cathedral, that I notice. My feet are bare.

I stand in front of the Cathedral with my eyes closed and the rain falling heavy on my face. I stretch my arms out wide like Jesus on the cross and pray.

Dear God,

Please, please help me!

Amen.

"You all right, love?" says a voice.

When I open my eyes a young man is peering at me through the pearly raindrops on his lashes, the radio thing in his pocket crackling and buzzing. I stare at him, blinking.

"Are you God?" I whisper, reaching my hand up and

touching his stubbly face.

He gently takes my arm. I flinch, remembering Tia's Dad's fat fists around my body. The policeman speaks into his radio, saying he's found a girl with no shoes on and I wonder who he's talking about.

"Where d'you live, sweetheart?" he says, leading me towards a police car. "What's your name?"

I snap myself together and my brain starts spinning. I can't tell him. I'll get Dad into trouble.

And where exactly do I live?

I don't even know the right answer any more.

"I'm Gabriella," I say, "and I'm trying to find my big brother, Beckett Midwinter. Do you know him?"

He speaks into his radio thing and puts a search out for Beckett.

"Sorry, Gabriella," he says, shaking his head, "we've got nothing on him. Where's your mum? It's too late for you to be out alone. We need to get you home, you're soaking."

Mum's face looms in my eyes as I reluctantly give him her address. Her evil shark teeth gnashing at me. I don't know what else to do. I've got nowhere else to go except to Henny and the police won't leave me with her.

I look up at the sky, through the glittering rain and wish a hand would come down and pluck me up and take me somewhere safe. The policeman bundles me into the car, my body moving like a puppet, hanging limply from a string.

"We'll have you home and dry in a flash," says a police lady with kind blue eyes, sliding in next to me.

I lean my head against the window and watch the raindrops dance through the sky as we drive up and down the streets. The car tyres swish through puddles, my breath makes steam on the glass. I see a big black car down a side road and Henny climbing inside. We pass the old warehouse building and I think about all the kids huddling on the rooftop, trying to stay dry. We pass Tia's and I wonder if she's sleeping.

"Where have you been, love?" says the police lady.

I turn to her. "I don't know," I say. "Everywhere, I'spose."

Chapter 18

When we get to Mum's I try clinging on to the minty feeling, but it slips from my grasp and this monster shark of fear clamps me in its jaws. The radio in the policeman's pocket crackles and hisses. He knocks on the door. My knees buckle under me and I have to grab the police lady's jacket to keep myself from falling to the ground.

"Mrs Midwinter?" she says, when Mum opens the door.

"Not any more! Why?" says Mum, peering at me like I was a really bad painting, pulling her purple dressing gown tightly round her sharp, skinny hips. "What do you want?"

"Well," says the policeman, "we found Gabriella out in the rain. She seems disorientated. She's soaked right through, needs a hot bath and something substantial to eat by all accounts."

Mum's face fades whiter than the moon, her eyes scanning me, piecing together paper-thin memories. Suddenly her hand flies out, grabs my sleeve and drags me inside. "Right," she snaps. "She'd better come in."

The door slams and me and Mum stand silently in the hallway for ages, staring at each other, our hearts thumping loudly in our chests. Then Mum flusters through to the kitchen, flapping wildly like a flag in the wind, and she fills the kettle with water then kicks the kitchen door shut.

"Nice of you to turn up out of the blue!" she hisses, shuffling through a pile of stuff in a drawer, pulling out a letter with Dad's handwriting on and jabbing it in my face.

"I had this pathetic letter from your dad land on my doormat, saying he was sending me a nice little surprise! I don't know what's been more worrying, the fact that you might be on your way here or the fact that you hadn't turned up. I've got a life of my own now, Gabriella. I've got kids, and a husband who knows nothing about *you!*"

She drops teabags into two blue cups and pours boiling water on top. She pulls the milk from the fridge, sniffs it, swills the carton around and then adds it to the tea. She puts two sugars in each cup, hands one to me and offers me a biscuit from the tin. And I don't know why, but my eyes fill up like water balloons about to burst as I cram the biscuit in my mouth.

"Well?" she says. "Where have you been? What've you got to say for yourself?"

I blow on my tea and watch a spiral of steam twirl towards the yellowy light bulb swinging from the dusty ceiling.

"Where's Beckett?"

"What do you mean – *where's Beckett?*" she says, taking a cigarette from a packet and lighting it. "What's he got to do with anything?"

"I've been trying to find him," I say quietly. "I thought he'd know what to do."

She takes a quick sip of tea. "Beckett's dead!" she

says. "Well, as far as I'm concerned he is, anyway. I washed my hands of *him* long ago."

My tummy drops to my knees; the water balloons burst and spill silently on to my cheeks. I hunt everywhere for that minty feeling, but it keeps on slipping away.

"Oh, don't start all that, Gabriella," Mum snaps, sucking hard on her cigarette, "for God's sake."

My lips tremble; I press the warm tea mug against them to try to keep them still. "Is he really..." I whisper, "is he really dead?"

Someone's feet thud down the stairs. The door flies open and Mum quickly shoves me behind it, squishing my face in the smelly towels hanging from a hook, slopping some of the scorching hot tea down my front.

"Who the crying out loud are you talking to at this time of night, woman?" says a voice.

"No one," says Mum, clattering her tea mug in the sink. "I can't sleep. I had the radio on."

The fridge opens; someone slurps and grunts, then slams it shut. The feet thud back up the stairs. Mum's hand drags me from behind the door; she pushes her face right up close to mine.

"You have no idea what kind of trouble you're going to get me into, do you?" she hisses. "Your dad agreed no contact and that was fine by me. He has a right cheek putting you on the train up here to barge back into my life uninvited, and I'll tell him so too when I get my hands on him!"

"Don't worry," I say, pulling away from her, blinking the tears from my eyes. "I can take care of myself. I only came here because of the policeman. I didn't want to!"

"Don't be ridiculous!" she whispers. "Even I wouldn't send you out on the streets! I'll put you in with the kids tonight and we'll talk about it in the morning. Connor's the top bunk, Jayda's the bottom. Climb in with her and cross your fingers she doesn't wet the bed. Thank your lucky stars Kev'll be off out to work early in the morning, so don't go showing your face until then. OK?"

We creep quietly up the stairs and Mum points me towards the bathroom. She hovers on the landing while I do a wee then shows me into the kids' room and goes off to bed. I can't see a thing; I have to feel my way around the room with one hand, careful not to spill the rest of my tea.

When my eyes get used to the dark I peep at Connor, lying with his mouth open wide under his Superman duvet, one little fist clinging on to his yellow bunny, the other shoved firmly in his mouth. I pull my wet clothes off and kick them under the bunks. Jayda is snoring gently, her arms stretched above her head; her chubby hands open wide like starfish. I ease my way in next to her, gently nudging her warm little body closer to the wall. Then I lean against the wooden bed end, sipping my tea, wondering what's going to happen to me next.

Chapter 19

When I wake up, Jayda's little body is wrapped around mine, her soft, warm baby breath tickling my ear.

"What you doing here?" says Connor, swinging his head down like a monkey and peering at me from the top bunk.

"Ssshhhh!" I say, opening my eyes. "We mustn't make a sound."

He snakes down, a yellow bunny ear clamped between his teeth, and wriggles in next to me.

"She'll need a wee soon," he says, pointing at Jayda and pinching his nose, "or she'll wet the bed."

"Let's make a tent," I whisper, sliding down the bed,

pulling Jayda's rainbow duvet up over our heads.

"But what are you doing here?" he says.

"I'll tell you later," I say, tugging his yellow bunny out of his mouth and making it skateboard up and down our legs.

"Have you ever been camping, Connor?"

He shakes his head.

"My friend Grace goes with her dad, sometimes," I whisper. "They go to Devon, somewhere near the sea. Shall we go together one day and watch the stars and sleep in a tent like this?"

Connor shoves his thumb in his mouth and snuggles up close. "Know any good stories?" he says.

Jayda wriggles, wraps her arms around my neck, sighs and drifts off back to sleep.

"What kind of stories do you like?" I whisper.

"Any ones," says Connor.

"Well," I say, as an idea floats into my mind, "once upon a time there was this boy who thought he was really rubbish at football."

Connor shrinks down the bed, sucking harder on his thumb. "What happened to him?" he whispers.

"Well," I say, "every time he tried to score a goal everyone laughed at him for being so bad. He felt like his feet were made of rubber because they were so bendy and squishy and wouldn't kick the ball straight."

"A bit like me," says Connor, his eyes twinkling in an arrow of light piercing through the tunnel of duvet.

"Then one day," I say, "a fairy came along…"

Connor laughs. He jabs my leg gently with his hot little foot. "Not fairies, silly," he says. "Fairies are for girls."

"Well, this was a special kind of fairy," I say. "He was this warrior fairy with war paint on his cheeks and special super-mega powers."

"OK, good," he smiles, nuzzling closer.

"Anyway, this special warrior fairy came along and sprinkled magic warrior dust all over the boy," I say. "You see, because everyone kept saying he was rubbish at football, he'd started to believe them. And he'd get more and more nervous when he played."

Jayda wriggles and sighs. A warm wet patch spreads across the bed and the strong smell of wee fills our noses. Connor's eyes flash like emergency sirens, painting his face with fear.

"I told you!" he hisses. "I told you she'd wet the bed!"

"Ssshhhh," I say. "It's OK! We need to be quiet. We mustn't move."

"But Mum'll go mad at me," he says. "She'll go mental."

I inch my legs away from the damp patch and find a dry spot for Connor. Clunks and thuds come from the next room. The growly man's voice mumbles. Someone flushes the toilet. Something grabs hold of my heart and squeezes it hard.

"Let's just ignore it for now and finish the story," I say, making a little air hole so we can breathe. "Anyway, once the magic dust touched the boy's skin he started to sparkle and fizz all over and all his worries about being rubbish at football began to melt away."

"Then what?" Connor says, rubbing the bunny's silky label between his finger and thumb.

"Well," I say, "the next time he played football the boy was amazing! His teacher was so astounded she gave him two hundred gold stars and put him in the football team. Then they won every single match they played and the boy became the best child player in the world!"

Connor giggles. "Then what?"

"Well, then what happened," I say, "was that when he grew up to be a big strong man, Manchester United football club signed him up and gave him twenty million pounds. And then he played for England in the World Cup final. It was the best football match the world had ever seen because he scored 150 goals. The other team didn't stand a chance and everyone loved him the best. They all kept saying he was amazing and brilliant. They said he was a hero and carried him round on their shoulders. And eventually he became the greatest man the world had ever known."

Connor lets out a gentle sigh and stretches he legs. "I wish it was true," he mumbles.

I pretend to sprinkle magic warrior fairy dust all over him. But then the front door slams. The motorbike roars away.

"We have to be quick," says Connor jumping up. "We have to get the sheets off before *she* comes in."

"Before *who* comes in?" says Mum, opening the bedroom door. "The cat's *mother*?"

Connor's eyes go as wide and round as the moon. He drags the duvet off the bed, pulls at the sheet. I jump up too. I lift Jayda to help him, little drops of wee dripping off her pyjamas like rain.

"Connor," shouts Mum, "you idiot! You know it's your job to get her up. Now I've got all this lot to deal with. You're useless, just like your father. And as for you Jayda…" she threatens.

"It was my fault," I say, feeling like a lioness with her cubs, "not theirs. I was trying to keep them quiet like you said. You don't have to worry, I'll sort it all out."

Memories come flooding into my mind like seawater into a cave. Memories of Beckett protecting me, of him being punished for stuff he didn't do.

"You go and have a cup of tea," I say to Mum. "I'll get Connor ready for school; I'll get Jayda sorted. I'll give them breakfast; you won't have to do anything."

Mum is stunned into silence. She shrugs her shoulders and fluffs back downstairs like a bird. I run into the bathroom, fill up the bath with warm bubbly water and lift Connor and Jayda in. I sit on the toilet seat, squeezing the flannel over them, making warm rivers rush down their soft pink skin. Jayda giggles; she splashes the bubbles with her palms, she empties beakers of water over her head. Connor reaches up and touches my face with his bath-wrinkly fingers.

"Are you the magic warrior fairy?" he says.

And I shake my head because I don't feel magic at all. I'm searching hard for the minty numb feeling, but my insides keep on thumping each other with huge great fists of fear, crashing together like angry waves.

Chapter 20

"Who is she?" asks Connor, when he's dressed for school and ready downstairs.

"Good question, Connor," Mum says, pressing the remote control, making the telly a bit louder. She's watching *Daybreak* and it reminds me of Dad. She puffs on her cigarette, blowing hazy blue smoke rings into the room. "Very good question," she says.

I head to the kitchen and pour cereal into bowls for Connor and Jayda. Jayda clings to my leg, babbling away in gobbledegook, smiling and sucking her fist. Connor slides on the sofa next to Mum, sticks his thumb in his mouth and stares at the telly with shiny, glazed eyes. I take him his breakfast and sit Jayda on the floor to feed her. She keeps grabbing my hair, splashing her fingers in the milk.

Mum rubs her hands together, digs a black wiggy bit of dirt from under her fingernail and flicks it on the floor. She looks at me. My heart leaps into my throat and burns.

"She's my niece," she says, winking at me. "That's it, Connor, she's your cousin and she's just popped by for a visit. Isn't that right, Gabriella?"

Connor waves at me, smiling. I stare at Mum in disbelief feeling like my skin is melting off my bones.

"But you don't have any brothers or sisters," I whisper, when Connor's lost in the telly again.

"Oh," Mum sneers, "you always were a bit of a Miss Smartypants, weren't you, Gabriella?"

"Just saying," I say, swallowing hard. "If I were your niece you'd have to have a brother or sister."

"Well, I don't know," she huffs. "Maybe I have, maybe they've just crawled out of the woodwork unexpectedly like you. The real question is, what am I going to do with you now? What am I going to tell Kev?"

"I told you last night," I whisper. "I'll just go. You don't have to worry about me."

I creep upstairs into the bathroom, undress and slip into Connor and Jayda's grey water. I never thought having a bath would feel this brilliant, even with scummy soap froth floating on top. It would be even better if Mum weren't downstairs being mean, calling me her *niece*.

I don't care about her anyway.

I hate her.

I slosh loads of shampoo in my hand, lather it up and stick my head under the hot tap to rinse it off. I need to make a plan. I need to know what happened to Beckett. I need to find him.

Mum's silent all the way to Connor's school. My clothes are still wet from last night's rain and feel weird because they're Tia's and don't really fit me very well. I find myself wrapping my sleeve around my hand like a bandage, like Tia does. Mum gave me an old pair of her trainers with red strips on. I hate them. They're too big and they're rubbing my heels.

Connor scoots in circles, peering at me from under

his fringe and smiling. Jayda babbles away in her pushchair, blowing kisses to everyone we pass.

I hate being with Mum. I remember her dragging me to school when I was small, me screaming, Beckett scurrying along to catch us up. I wish I could run away and forget all about her, forget that she ever existed.

I try to make a plan for if I don't find Beckett, but it only takes me back to Henny and Tia. I like being family with Henny, but I wish we could live in a real house together. I wish I were a grown-up and could get a job and take care of myself. I wish I didn't have to be here.

When we get back to Mum's house she puts the kettle on, slumps back on the sofa and stares at me.

"You've got those sheets to be getting on with, Missy."

I gather Jayda into my arms and take her up the stairs with me. I bundle up her sheets, find clean ones in the airing cupboard and make her bed all pretty and fresh with a line of cuddly teddies. Jayda squeals with laughter, climbs under the covers and smiles this big smile that makes my heart feel as warm as the sun. I slide in next to her.

"I'm actually your big sister, Jayda," I whisper, "not Mum's niece. And as well as Connor, we have this really big brother called Beckett. He's lovely. Really lovely. That means there's four of us, which means we're a big family."

I count four fingers to show her then brush bits of food and Lego blocks and plastic men out of Connor's bed, making his all neat and tidy too. I play *This little piggy went to market* with Jayda and then set up her post-box toy and we take turns posting the shapes into the holes, clapping each other and laughing when we get it right. "Again, again, again," she squeals.

We're just about to start playing puzzles when Mum appears at the door.

"I've been thinking," she says, leaning against the doorframe. "You could help me with the kids. And we'd get extra benefit too. It mightn't be such a bad idea."

Jayda wriggles her chubby toes. I try to swallow, but I can't.

"What will you say to Kev?" I ask.

"I'll tell him you're my niece," she says. "He's so useless he won't put two and two together. I'll say you're an orphan or something."

I twiddle a colourful puzzle piece in my hand. "Please tell me about Beckett," I say.

"Oh, you and your Beckett," she snaps, "Beckett this, Beckett that! Gabriella, you're giving me a headache."

"But where is he?" I say. "I thought he came to live with you. I stayed with Dad and he came with you. What happened? You have to tell me!"

Mum huffs. "I told you last night," she says. "As far as I'm concerned, he's dead, so do me a favour and give over asking, will you?"

I wish I could pick Jayda up and race to Connor's school and get him. I wish we could run away to somewhere kind and lovely and safe. I wish we had a granny or an auntie or someone special like that to go to. I wish we could go to Grace's mum.

I wish someone bigger could help.

Mum tells me I have to take Jayda and get Connor from school because she has a headache. I settle her in her bedroom with some headache pills and a big mug of tea. Then I pack a little picnic to take to the park and slip a football in a bag. Jayda babbles and chuckles in her pushchair, and even though the word *niece* digs into me like a splinter I feel happier for the first time in forever.

"I'll take care of you," I say to Jayda, while we're waiting at the gates. "I won't let her be mean to you any more. I promise. I'll be your mummy, or kind of mummy-ish big sister."

When Connor comes into the playground he's waving this picture of a boat proudly in his hand and beaming with excitement. I stoop down and talk to him about it for ages. He says it's a pirate boat going to a treasure island. He shows me the pirates inside and says it's me and Jayda and him. I roll his picture up and tuck it safely in the basket under Jayda's seat.

"It's brilliant, Connor," I say, smiling at the splodgy, wobbly shapes on the page. "We'll find a special place on the wall for it."

In the park we sit on the roundabout and eat cheese sandwiches and crisps and sip squash from a bottle that dribbles down our chins. I imagine I'm Grace's mum, all smiley and gentle. I wish I had money to buy white chocolate Magnums for us all. I wish there was a special place where we could dangle our feet in cool green water and watch the moorhens nesting.

We stay in the park for ages, spinning and sliding and swinging higher and higher, until we can see the rooftops shining in the sun. When Jayda falls asleep in her pushchair with a sweet, sticky grin on her face, Connor and me get the football out. We play for hours until our feet are sore, until Connor has scored five goals, until my heart is full to the brim with love for them both.

Chapter 21

Mum opens the front door to let us in, and her eyes are black with fury. Then Dad's fat red sunburnt face appears behind her.

"Dad?" I say, clinging on to the blue pushchair handles. "What are you doing here?"

"Good question," spits Mum. "As if it wasn't bad enough having you arrive on my doorstep without *him* turning up as well!"

We tumble into the front room and I'm trembling inside like a mouse under the glare of a cat. Jayda strains on her pushchair harness, trying to launch herself at a great pile of toys in the corner. Connor stays quietly next to me, his sweaty little hand clutching mine. Dad slumps on the sofa, picking at his blistered skin. Mum huffs into the kitchen.

"This sunburn is killing me," Dad says. "You'd never believe how hot it was out there."

I don't answer him. I'm swirling with confusion.

Mum huffs in with some tea, slamming the cups on the table. She unwraps a packet of biscuits, spraying sparkles of sugar all over the floor. She slumps on the sofa next to Dad and hits the remote, sparking the telly into life. Dad turns his body away from her and sighs. He crosses his arms and rests them on his fat belly as if it were a shelf. Mum does the same.

And I stand there feeling invisible.

Just like I always did. Just like forever.

"You got us into a right old mess, Gabriella," Dad says, his eyes pleading. "If you'd hadn't annoyed Amy so much with not tidying your room and stuff she might have let you come to the wedding. You might never have had to come up here in the first place. You could've come on holiday! Best we pack your things and get you back home ASAP."

"But what about the flat?" I say, kneeling on the floor and sipping my tea. "What about the rent?"

Mum's ears prick up. She twitches her head from side to side not sure if the telly is more interesting than what's being said. Dad shrinks back.

"Trust me, it's all sorted, Gabriella," he says, his eyes searching for something safe to land on. "We're camping out at Amy's mum's house for a bit until we get back on our feet. I've got my fingers in a few pies, job-wise, and something smashing will come up soon, I'm sure of it. Her mum's got a nice place near the swimming pool on Stonebridge."

"So it's all looking up for *you* then, Dave!" Mum snaps. "Not like some of us, stuck in this dump with two more kids and another rubbish husband."

Dad holds his hands over his mouth and rubs his chin. I wish I could run out of here with Connor and Jayda right now.

"Well," he says, looking at me, "things *are* on the up, I promise. But right now I'm in a little spot of trouble, Gabriella, and we need to get ourselves back home quick."

I feel like I'm sliding, like the room's been tipped up and everything's slipping away. "What kind of trouble?" I ask, fiddling with my too-long sleeve.

"It's school," says Dad. "They're all up in arms about me not telling them you'd come to your mum's place. I just never got round to calling them. They sent the police over and everything. Amy did her nut! And I tried to call you, Gabriella, loads of times. Why didn't you answer your phone?"

"I didn't have the charger," I say. "You forgot to pack it!"

"But where have you *been*?" he asks, slurping his tea and snatching a peek at the telly. "Mum says you only just got here. Where were you all this time, Gabriella? I sent you off with clear instructions to find your way to Mum's."

"Where were *you*, Dave, more like?" snaps Mum. "*You're* supposed to be her father, *you're* the one that's supposed to know where she is! And what did you expect me to do with her anyway? Kev knows nothing about her!"

Then they both look at me like I'm the one who's

done something wrong.

"I don't know where I've been," I say, twisting my jumper sleeve. "Everywhere. Nowhere."

Jayda tips the toybox up, sending thousands of plastic shapes skittering across the floor.

"Come on then, Gabriella," says Dad, rising from the sofa. "I'm not standing any more of this nonsense. Let's get out of here, shall we?"

Connor scurries over and grabs my hand, squeezing it tight, pleading with his eyes for me to stay.

"I'm not sure you're fit to take her," snaps Mum. "I think she should stay with me now. Right little gem she's been today, helping out with the kids. And the extra cash from Social Services'll come in handy, I can tell you!"

Dad's voice gets louder. "She's coming with me," he says, pointing his finger at Mum, "and there's nothing you can do about it. Anyway, you're hardly the model mother, are you?"

Then he looks at me. "Come on, Gabriella," he says. "Once we get settled in our new place you and me can cosy up and watch telly together while Amy's out at

Zumba class. We'll watch out for another one of those eclipse things if you like. It'll be lovely, just like old times, I promise."

"Don't go!" whispers Connor, pressing himself against me. "I like you here. I need more of that magic dust."

I stand in the middle of the room, totally invisible, while my parents start to fight like cats, my brain spinning faster than a fairground ride. I might as well not be here. This argument has nothing to do with me. It's all about them and what they need.

I'm pulled to Mum because of Connor and Jayda and I'm pulled to Dad because he looks so sad. But I don't want either of them.

"Where's Beckett?" I say. "I need to know!"

Mum switches the telly over and presses her hands to her ears, making a *lalalalaing* noise like she can't hear me.

"You don't understand," I shout. "I need to *see* him!"

Jayda starts whimpering, toddles over and clings on to my leg. I sit on the floor and pull both of the kids on to my lap.

"What in the Lord's name has Beckett got to do with anything?" laughs Dad.

"Don't you want to see him too, Dad?" I ask. "Don't you want to see your own son while you're here?"

Dad twists his head round like a clockwork toy to face me.

"Oh, Gabriella," he says, rubbing his face with his palms. "He's not my son, love. Mum already had him when we met. He's nothing to do with me! Didn't we tell you that already?"

Something snaps inside me. I search for the minty feeling, but everything keeps snapping and breaking and cracking like an ancient tree in the wind. My head starts swimming with noise, the ground starts shifting beneath me again, like the floor will open up and we'll all go tumbling down.

I cling on to Jayda and Connor, feeling their soft, warm breath on my cheeks and their hearts pounding fast in my ears. I'm not leaving them with Mum. *I'm not!* I don't care what anyone says. I'm going to stay with them until I'm old enough to take care of them myself.

Dad gets up and towers over me. Connor stares at him with frightened rabbit eyes. Jayda stuffs her thumb in her mouth and sucks.

"Gabriella," he says, "listen to me, will you? It's time to go!"

"Oh, my! Look at Mr Big Man," says Mum, standing up and taunting him. "No one's ever listened to you before, Dave, so why do you think they'll start listening now?"

Mum and Dad stand in front of each other, their eyes yellow with poison, their hot tongues licking each other with fire.

"So stop me then," Dad seethes. "I'll have you over the coals with Social Services in no time." He casts his hand over the toppling piles of mess in the room. "Just look at this place," he hisses. "It's disgusting in here. Needs a public health warning!"

Dad grabs my arm and pulls me up, scattering the kids, leaving them struggling like frightened ants. Then Mum's there, grabbing the other arm, and I'm five again, in the middle of their fight, being ripped in half like a piece of Henny's bubblegum.

"I don't want either of you," I screech, crumpling on the floor with my head in my hands. "I don't want either of you. I just want Beckett!"

With all the noise no one hears the motorbike roar up or the front door squeak open.

But we all hear it slam.

And then we all hold our breath and freeze.

"Hello, hello, hello," says Kev, scratching his beard, looking round the room. "What the bucket of roses is going on here?"

Mum slumps down on the sofa, switches the telly up even louder and ignores him. Dad ignores him too. He picks up another biscuit and snaps it in half, spraying crumbs through the air. Connor scrabbles back on my lap, pressing his face close up to my ear. Kev grunts that he's starving hungry and shuffles into the kitchen.

"Right," hisses Dad, yanking on my arm. "Enough of this malarkey, young lady."

I've turned into a rag doll with no stuffing left inside me. Jayda clambers on to my lap. She covers my face with dribbly kisses that are so loving I'd like to scoop them up and keep them safely in a scrapbook forever.

Mum gathers the tea things and shuffles into the kitchen after Kev. Connor presses his face even closer to my ear, twiddling my hair through his sticky fingers.

"I know Beckett," he whispers and my heart stops, "He comes to my school to say hello. I do know him. He gave me Yellow Bunny."

My breath catches in my throat.

"Go and start the car, Dad," I say, "I'll be out in a minute."

I stare at Connor. His eyes twinkle with hope.

"Tell him I've been here," I whisper, "next time he comes to school. Tell him I've been here and that now I'm back with my dad and I'm living near the swimming pool. Please tell him, Connor, *please*!"

Chapter 22

We climb into Dad's car and drive along in silence, making our way out of the city, on to the long ribbons of motorway. I can't stop worrying about Connor and Jayda, about leaving them in Manchester with Mum. I can't stop thinking about Beckett.

"What did happen to Beckett, Dad?" I ask, at last. "Why won't Mum talk about him?"

"Search me," shrugs Dad. "How in heaven's name should I know, or even care for that matter? He's nothing to do with me."

Dad's words dig into my skin. Why doesn't anyone care about Beckett but me?

"All right, Gabriella?" says Amy, when we get to her mum's.

She's stretching out on a sun lounger, soaking up the warmth of the late summer evening. "Get me a drink will you, babe," she says to Dad, wiggling her wedding ring finger in the air so the golden band glows. "Then we can light the little garden lanterns, can't we? And make everything all romantic like."

I ignore Amy and sit on her mum's white plastic back-door step, watching a little fat bumblebee darting in and out of a flower. I wish I had my paper and my pens. I'd like to draw that bee heading over towards Amy to sting her.

"I've made up a camp bed for you in the little back room, princess," says Amy's mum, flitting about with a yellow duster in her hand. "Now, where are your things? You're probably tired out after that long journey of yours."

"I don't have any stuff," I say, kicking Mum's trainers off. "I lost it all."

Amy's ears prick up. "Lost it all, Gabriella?" she

shrieks. "What are you talking about?"

I begin to search for the minty feeling inside, but her stony glare sends it running for cover. The burning arrows firing from her eyes scorch the soft bit in the middle of my bones.

I shrug. "I just lost it," I say, swallowing hard.

"Oh, *Dave!*" she says, flapping her arms about. "I told you it was a big mistake getting her back. You should have kept your trap shut and left things how they were." Her eyes pin me to the spot. "Well, if you think we're going to rush out and buy you a load of new stuff, Gabriella, you've got another think coming! You should've been more careful."

"How can you have just lost it all?" sighs Dad. "What d'you mean, just lost it? It was in a blimming big bag!"

"I just did."

"You've got your uniform, though, right?" says Dad, stripping off his shirt and flumping down on a garden chair, his lobster-red tummy quivering like jelly. "You've got that, haven't you?"

I shake my head.

"Oh, for crying out loud, Gabriella," he says. "What

did you do with it?"

I sit there in silence, staring at the shadow on the path, vivid images swirling.

My school uniform, those ridiculous big PE knickers stuffed in the train carriage bin.

My A* schoolbooks sloshing down the toilet. Colin's leering snow face.

The laptop lady's soft hands tapping.

The smell of the *No Fear* skateboarder's pasty.

The busker girl with the guitar I wanted to hide in, the coins in her hat glinting in the sunlight.

The silky black tattoo angel wings.

Henny, her stripy pink hair and dark smudgy eyes.

Kingdom, swooshing up and down in his big black car.

Tia wrapping herself in her long sleeves, resting her sad, thin face on her knees.

The black gungy bin with the slimy ketchup and the stolen tiara winking at me.

The little brown dog weeing.

Tia's dad's big fat fists squishing me.

And those voices flying from the Cathedral like doves.

"It's been the long day," says Amy's mum, staring at her watch. "The nights will start drawing in soon." She picks up a green plastic watering can and gives her flowers a shower. She takes a dead head from a rose, pulls a slug off a cabbage and tuts. "I s'pose it's all downhill to winter."

Amy's mum finds me a nightdress with little purple flowers on it and itchy frills round the neck. She runs me a shoulder-deep lavender bubble bath and bustles in with hot chocolate for me. I cover myself with the flannel and she smiles and fills a white plastic jug with water to wash my hair even though I can do it myself.

"Never mind, princess," she says, tucking me into the little wobbly camp bed, after she's brushed and dried my hair. "It'll all work out. It always does. I promise."

When I'm just about to fall asleep Dad pops his head round the door.

"Night then," he says, leaning on the doorframe, checking his big fat tummy in the mirror on the wall.

"Why did you bring me back, Dad?" I whisper. "Why did you bother? Why didn't you just leave me there with Mum and Connor and Jayda?"

Dad shrugs his shoulders, his tummy wobbling under their weight.

"The police, I s'pose," he says. "I don't want to get locked up, Gabriella, do I? Not for something as stupid as this! Plus, if the truth be told, I couldn't stand the guilt of it. It niggled away too much."

When Dad leaves the room I wipe away a sneaky tear. I'd have quite liked it if he'd said he missed me, or something nice like that.

I lie in the little camp bed listening. Amy's voice slides under the door like a snake. The telly sounds vibrate through the walls. An owl in a nearby tree hoots. Fighting cats yowl and screech on the fence. The late night car tyres swish by.

Amy's mum's sheets are soft on my face, the pillow like marshmallow. And for the first time in ages I'm in a clean bed with a glass of water on the table by my side. And Grace's mum is round the corner. Slowly, slowly, sleep creeps in and covers me in velvet.

Amy's mum wakes me early with a cup of tea and four bourbon biscuits. I put Tia's clothes on and we slip out of the house without waking up Dad. We drive to Sainsbury's and she picks out some new school uniform things for me, a pair of pyjamas, two T-shirts, some long-sleeved tops, some jeans and three dresses.

"Dad doesn't have the money for them," I say, nervously twisting a tissue in my hands. "He won't be able to pay you back."

Amy's mum smiles and throws some oranges in the trolley, a packet of Shreddies, some strawberry yogurts and fresh crusty bread. She buys a special snack-pack with ham and cheese for my lunch and some crisps and a chocolate cupcake and a carton of fresh juice with bits in, not squash.

She grabs some sparkly hair bobbles from the swing-around stand, some white socks, a pack of different coloured knickers with butterflies on, some black pumps and a cute little necklace with a silvery heart.

"I don't have any grandchildren of my own, yet," she whispers, her eyes twinkling as she throws two chocolate eclairs into the trolley and a big bottle of lemonade for later. "So I don't see why I shouldn't spoil you instead."

Then it's like she can't stop herself. She throws a

Mizz mag in the trolley and this amazing purple watch with pretend diamonds on it and some bangles. She lets me choose a new pencil case and I get a blue denim one with little red flowers embroidered all over it.

And a new pack of pencils and felt tip pens.

I wonder if Amy had this much stuff when she was small.

At McDonald's we huddle in the toilets getting me changed for school. Amy's mum brushes my hair, battling with my unruly curls. We eat Egg McMuffins for breakfast and we don't talk much and it's lovely, just being together, without her asking questions. I slide along the seat so our arms almost touch while we chew.

When we get to my old school, Dad's pacing up and down outside the gates like a tiger in a cage. My heart dips. My mouth goes dry.

"Where you been?" he says, grabbing my arm. "I've been doing my pieces here, waiting."

Amy's mum takes charge.

"We went to buy uniform, didn't we Gaby?" she says, looking Dad up and down with disappointment flickering in her eyes. "Someone had to, Dave!"

Dad wipes the sweat from his face.

"Right. Well. Thanks, then," he says, shifting from one foot to another. "Come on, Gabriella, let's get this over and done with, shall we? Let's face the music with that headmaster of yours."

We walk to the school office in silence, our hearts hammering. Then Dad goes inside with the headmaster and the school secretary sends me off to class.

"Gabriella!" calls Grace, bounding across the playground like a puppy in the park. "You're back!"

Chapter 23

"**W**here did you go?" whispers Grace, during Science while we're testing the temperature of the water in our polystyrene cup.

I don't know how to answer. There's so much to tell, but nothing she'd understand. And if she tells her mum then my dad might get in trouble with the police.

"I told you. I went to my mum's."

"Then why are you back?" she says, writing the temperature on our results table.

I wish I could spill everything out. I wish I could tell her about Henny and Tia, sleeping on the warehouse roof with the sounds of the city blaring below and the huge blue moon shining on my drawings. I wish I could tell her about the fire in the shop and the diamonds of glass shattering all over the ground. I wish I could tell her how much the blood raced round my body when I broke into the apartment so Henny could steal things. And that a big black car chases me through the night in my dreams; hiding in the shadows, waiting to catch me.

"Dad changed his mind," I say. "He came back for me."

I pour boiling water into a glass beaker and watch the wispy steam rise. Grace's curtain of hair falls in front of her face and she tucks it behind her ear so she can write numbers on our chart neatly.

"Zoe's mum says the police are involved," she says. "That they're after your dad for taking you out of school for so long."

I shake my head and use my new pencils to colour in our graph. Grace tells me about a sleepover she had with Zoe and Elsie at the weekend. She tells me all about the film they watched and the milkshakes they made that spilt everywhere. And that they couldn't stop laughing. She talks non-stop and I like hearing the sound of her voice again. And I don't know why, but I feel like crying.

After school Zoe comes racing over and threads her arm through Grace's. They kind of pull in, close together, in a way that makes me ache.

"I'm so excited!" Zoe says, her eyes glittering in the sunlight. Zoe's all glittery and shimmery everything.

I feel in my hair and touch the glittery bobbles Amy's mum bought me from Sainsbury's. And then Grace's mum pulls up in her red car. She winds down the window and turns her soft face right towards us, so we can see the whole of it, her red lips and everything, smiling. And my heart pounds so I put my hand on my chest in case she hears.

"We're going swimming," says Grace, touching my wrist. "We planned it yesterday. I didn't know… I didn't know you'd be back otherwise I'd have invited you. But we'll go soon, yeah?"

They climb into the car, all girl legs and arms, and clunk the door shut. I hear their seatbelts click in place. Grace's mum looks at me. She smiles and blows me a kiss and I hold my breath while it travels on the breeze to my cheek.

And then she says, "Ready, girls?" And they drive away.

Mrs Evans rushes over to me.

"I'm glad I caught up with you," she says, looping a long, rainbow-coloured silk scarf around her neck. "Is everything OK, Gabriella? We were so worried about you when you disappeared."

A lump grows in my throat. All the words I can't say, pressing hard to get out.

I nod, keeping my eyes on a little train of ants creeping along the pavement. I don't trust myself to look at her in case her kind eyes make me cry or blurt stuff out.

"I went to my mum's," I say. "Dad forgot to let the school office know."

"You would say though," she says, fixing the big brass buckle on her bag. "You know, you would tell me if something was wrong, wouldn't you?"

"Nothing's wrong," I say, feeling suddenly annoyed by Mrs Evans. "I'm OK."

I walk back to Amy's mum's house slowly, wishing I could've gone swimming with Grace and then back to her house for tea. If I could've chosen, I'd have had her mum's creamy fish pie and peas. I'd have borrowed Grace's flowery bikini, the one she got at the airport when she was on her way to Greece.

I'm scared of seeing Dad, or scared that the police have taken him away. I sit on a bench in the park and listen to the traffic climbing the hill. I wish Tia were around, or even Henny. I feel too sad just sitting here alone.

"Hello," says the cupcake lady, plopping down on the bench. "I'm glad to see you again. Haven't seen you around for ages. Fancy a cupcake? I've a few left and if I eat them all myself I'll end up as big as a whale!"

I take a cupcake with yellow swirly icing and butterflies on top. I don't really want a cupcake; I want fish and peas and salty things. But I don't want her to think I'm rude. So I nibble round the edge while she munches up a white one covered in a million silver balls.

The park lady talks and talks and talks and I don't even have to answer. She tells me about her day and her

dog and her grandchildren
vegetable patch. She tells
come into the park at e
coffee and how she's a
all go when the winter settles i

I think about Manchester then an
the kids go at night when it gets really cold.
tells me she makes these novelty cakes for people
birthdays and special occasions and that her son-in-law
is building her a website to get the word round. And her
voice is like the longest train; it goes on and on forever.

"Well," she says, at last, brushing cake crumbs off
her lap and pushing another cupcake into my hands.
"I best be off. Milo will be expecting his walk. See you
again."

"Bye," I say, wishing she'd stay longer, wishing I
could rest my head on her soft arm and go to sleep.

At Amy's mum's they're all in the garden and Dad's
pretending to spray Amy with the hosepipe. Amy's
squealing for him to stop because she doesn't want
to get her clothes wet, but anyone can tell she doesn't
really mean it.

happened at school, Dad?" I whisper. "...d they say? Did the police come? Are you in ...e?"

"...h, don't go on, Gabriella," he says. "We're having ...! They'll get over their little tantrum now you're back. Why don't you go and do your homework or something?"

I sit on the wobbly camp bed and rest my new Geography book on my knees. I'm supposed to be writing about settlements, but my head's racing so much it's hard to concentrate. I can't believe I'm back sitting in a bedroom, doing my homework whilst everything's still going on in Manchester. I wish Amy's mum could make a nice big pot of something tasty and we could drive it up there to feed Tia and everyone else. I think about Tia and her hairy dad and my tummy flips over like a pancake. I can't believe Dad and Amy are actually married, that she's officially my step-mum. I'll never call her that, not ever. I wonder how many homeworks I missed while I was away. I wonder how much other stuff I missed.

A settlement is a place where people live. It can

232

be a house on its own or a hamlet, a village, a town or a large city. Nearly all settlements started as hamlets or villages.

Settlements make me think about Manchester again. About all the kids huddling together, making a village of their own. I wonder how many street kids it would take to make a city.

Amy's mum makes sausage and mash with onion gravy for our tea. We balance it on our laps and watch *EastEnders* together while Dad and Amy go to the pub. Then she runs me a lavender bubble bath and I stay in it, shoulder deep, until my fingertips go chalk-white and wrinkly.

She brings me hot chocolate, and when I'm in my new pyjamas I dig another cupcake out of my bag. It's a bit squashed, but I tell her about the park lady not wanting to be a whale and Amy's mum laughs. We share the cake while she sits on the edge of the camp bed and reads me three chapters of this book called *The Painted Garden*. I lie on the soft pillow and melt into her voice that flows out of her mouth like a lullaby.

When she's pecked me on the cheek and snapped off the light I close my eyes and don't let myself think even for one minute about Beckett or Blue Bunny.

Chapter 24

One week ago

On Saturday, while Dad and Amy are at the shops, Amy's mum and I sit in the garden making strings of pretty beads into bracelets. She got these teensy beads and you have to thread the thin elastic stuff on to a needle, tie a knot and feed the little beads on. They remind me of those hundreds and thousands things the park lady puts on her cupcakes; there are so many colours. We've got some tiny silver charms too and some bigger glass beads that twinkle and sparkle in the sun, making rainbows on my hands. I have six bracelets jingling on my wrist already.

Amy's mum is telling me that after the beads we'll have a snack and another few chapters of *The Painted Garden*, when all of a sudden there's this big bang on the door. I don't really think much about it because it's not my house. I just carry on threading while Amy's mum goes to answer it. Then I hear this deep voice and a rush of feet and I panic that it's the police after Dad.

So when I look up I can't believe my eyes.

I have to blink a few times in case I'm imagining things.

There is a man standing there, just standing there in Amy's mum's garden, with the washing flapping near his ear.

The face in the little photo Dad forgot to put in my backpack flashes through my brain, flickering and moving, slipping and sliding. I look up at the man in front of me then back at the photo image in my mind.

My heart is clattering like mad.

The man in the garden has a stubbly chin.

He has this crazy, wild hair.

And it's not until I notice he's clutching Blue Bunny

tightly in his hand that I know for sure that the complete miracle standing in front of me is Beckett.

It is actually him.

And seeing him here, just knowing he's alive and real makes me crackle all over. It makes my chest fill up with the hugest pressure of everything. And Beckett just stands there, smiling, looking at me as if I were a complete miracle too.

"Hey," he says, with this big grin on his face, "I found you!"

He holds Blue Bunny out to me, tipping his head slightly to one side like he always did. "I found *him* too," he smiles, waggling him in the air. "In Selfridges. I thought you might be missing him."

My heart's banging in my throat and there's this ringing sound in my ears. I stand up. I stretch my hand out to Blue Bunny and every part of me wants to fly into Beckett's arms.

"Beckett!" I croak. "Beckett!"

Amy's mum quietly nods then leaves us in the garden alone, and I turn into a volcano, all the boiling hot lava inside me gushing out. I tell Beckett about Dad and

Amy; about Grace's mum's garden shed; about Colin on the train and everything in Manchester. I tell him all about Mum and Connor and Jayda and my eyes turn into a river too and I can't stop crying.

Beckett listens quietly, holding me in his golden-eyed gaze until my talking stops. Then he stands up and pulls some papers out of his brown jacket pocket. He swishes them through the air like a sword.

"Listen to me carefully, Gabriella," he says. "I've got something important to tell you. I got an Emergency Care Order, which means you're safe. We'll need to jump through more hoops to make it permanent, but everyone assures me we'll get there. You never have to live with Mum or your dad again. Not ever. You're coming to live with me. I'm going to take care of you."

A lady I don't know peeps her face out of the back door and smiles.

"It's true, Gabriella," she says. "I'm Lizzie. I'm your Social Worker and I've come with Beckett to get you. We have everything in writing."

I can't say a word. So many things are crashing around inside me I think I might explode.

Why have I got a Social Worker? How come I didn't know?

Beckett tugs a strand of messy hair from his eyes. Amy's mum comes into the garden and takes the papers from Beckett. She looks at them carefully, reading every single word. Her face looks really serious and sad, and for a minute I think Beckett's got it wrong.

Then she looks up at me and nods. "What about it, princess?" she says.

A million yeses are sitting on my tongue, screaming to be heard, but I can't seem to spit them out. Beckett comes so close I can smell him. He's this friendly mix of wood smoke and spice. He rests the palm of his hand on my back.

"I never forgot about you, Gabriella," he says. "I've been waiting for this day. I've been waiting for you forever."

I can't move. Everything is thrumming all over.

"Is this what you want, Gaby?" says Amy's mum, taking my hand. "Because if it is, you'd better get moving."

"But what about Dad?" I say, panicking.

"But what about *you*, Gabriella?" says Beckett. "This is your chance to do something good for *you*. Mum and your dad don't really care about anything but themselves. They never really have. They've never really seen us, Gabriella, they've never thought about what *we* need. We might as well have been invisible. So it's time to think of yourself, Gabriella, to work out what you need for you."

I jingle the bracelets on my wrist and sit back down on a stripy garden chair because my legs are weak with worry.

"I looked everywhere for you," I say, sniffing back my tears, remembering the wet mirror puddles in the street. "Everywhere."

"I know," he says, kneeling down and taking my hand, "I know. And I'm so sorry you couldn't find me. I was there all along. Just round the corner."

"Do you really want me to come?" I ask. "Because it's OK if you don't. I don't mind."

He pulls a scruffy leather wallet from his pocket, opens it and shows me a photo of a little girl with untameable brown hair.

"Who's that?" I ask. "Have you got a daughter?"

Beckett laughs. "No, silly, it's you! I've carried this with me every day since Mum and I left. I vowed to myself that one day I'd come and find you."

He looks shy for a moment, then he coughs and says, "I *want* you to come with me, Gabriella. I always have. I was just too young to do anything about it before now."

I suck the warm air deep into my lungs, hold it there for a minute while my brain cogs turn everything round, and then let it all out in a rush.

"OK," I say, my body flooding with relief. "I'll come."

Amy's mum flies into action, gathering my stuff up and neatly folding it into a pretty bag with daisies on. She makes everyone a cup of tea. My heart is hammering so loud. We have to wait for Dad. Amy's mum puts her arms around me and pulls me so close that my nose touches her powdery neck. She takes my face between her gentle hands and fixes her watery grey eyes on mine.

"You be a good girl, OK?" she says, tears spilling from the corners of her eyes. "Be a good girl for your brother and never let anyone hurt you again. And remember that everything that happened wasn't your fault. You didn't do anything wrong, Gabriella. They were the parents; it was their job to look after you, not the other way round."

Amy's mum slips the bracelet making stuff in my bag along with *The Painted Garden*.

"I don't think I'll be able to talk to Dad," I say, my voice splintering like wood. "I can't…"

I pull out a sheet of paper and in blue pencil I write a letter for Dad to read when I've gone.

Dear Dad,

I'm sorry if I hurt you, but I had to go. I'm making a fresh start with Beckett.

You've got Amy now, so I know you'll be OK.

I do love you,

Gabriella XXX

Chapter 25

When Dad and Amy get back from the shops I freeze. Lizzie sits up very straight in the chair. She coughs, quietly. Amy's mum gathers the teacups, gently squeezes my shoulder and disappears into the kitchen.

Beckett takes my hand and I can feel his heartbeat through his skin.

"What in the name of sunshine is going on here, then?" says Dad, popping his fat, wobbly tummy through the doorway.

"We're leaving," says Beckett.

"Oh, right, I see," smirks Dad. "You're barely out of nappies yourself, boy. Who do you think you are, coming in here and throwing your weight around?"

"That's right, Dave," says Amy, barging forward with arms full of shopping bags. "You tell him."

She peers at Beckett.

"And who in heaven's name are you, anyway?"

"I'm Gabriella's brother," says Beckett, pulling the Emergency Care Order out of his pocket and thrusting it in Dad's face. "And it's legal. I've got every right to be here."

Then Lizzie stands up, shakes Dad's hand and tells him all about the law and everything. Dad leans back with his mouth wide open, looking like someone has just pulled all the soft purply bits inside him out and laid them on the table in front of him. I'm holding on tight to Beckett, keeping my eyes down, with this big guilty feeling eating huge chunks out of my heart. I'm praying that Dad won't look at me, wishing Beckett and I could just make ourselves invisible and slide away unnoticed.

But he does.

His eyes land on me and feel sticky and heavy on my skin.

"You're not really going, are you, Gabriella?" he says, his voice fading away, like it does when Amy shouts at him. "You're not really going to leave me, are you?" And I'm five years old again. Hating feeling so small and weak, wishing I were as tall and as strong as a tree so I could prop Dad up and kiss his hurts better. I flick my eyes up to meet his and they kill me with all the sadness swimming inside them.

"I have to, Dad," I croak. "I'm sorry, but I have to go."

Dad stumbles, his knees buckling. He flops into a chair, his cheeks sagging because he knows there's nothing more to say.

We climb into Lizzie's car and Beckett sits in the back next to me. He clicks my seatbelt in and I dig my hand deep in my pocket and hold on to Blue Bunny's ear. I look at Amy's mum's house, and Dad's there with his face pressed against the window, steam from his breathing smudging around him.

Lizzie puts the radio on. It's a song called *I Know You Care*. And I feel so shy being next to Beckett and yet every part of me knows him like not even a day has gone past since he left.

"How did you find me?" I whisper.

"Long story," he smiles. "I was in Selfridges with my girlfriend, Leila, looking at bridesmaid dresses for her friend's wedding. And Blue Bunny was just sitting there by the till looking so lost and alone. Leila asked the shop assistant how he got there and she said someone had dropped him. She decided to leave him by the till in case someone came looking for him. Then a few days later I was lying in bed and it suddenly hit me – he was yours.

"I couldn't make sense of it at first. I mean why would your Blue Bunny be in Manchester? But I got up and ran straight back to the shop as fast as I could. I remembered I'd drawn the heart on his chest and my name on his label. And there it was. Something told me you needed me more than ever."

"And then what happened next?" I say.

"Well," he says, "I visit Connor at school every week to check he's OK. We chat through the fence and I give him sandwiches and stuff. He said you'd been at Mum's, looking for me. That every time you saw him, you asked him if he knew me. He said now you'd gone back with your dad and he was to tell me that you were living near the swimming pool. I went straight to Social Services. They had Amy's mum's address because they were on to your dad for negligence already. He should never have left you on your own, Gabriella."

I feel bad about Dad. The word *negligence* makes something thump and twist in my chest. I think about his fat wobbly tummy and Amy poking it. I think of him pushing the vacuum round, doing his exercises. I know he didn't mean to hurt me. I know he didn't really want it to be like this. He would've watched another eclipse with me one day. I know deep down that he wanted to.

We stop in town to get a drink and a snack and then drive the long ribbony motorways back to Manchester, talking about everything in the world. I'm still finding it hard to believe that Beckett wanted me to come and live with him all this time.

There are things about us that are the same, but others that are different. Beckett likes drawing too, but he's not much into telly. He lives on the canal; he shows me photos on his phone of his narrow boat. It's called *Providence* and it's all red and green paint and shiny brass.

He shows me photos of his girlfriend, Leila, and I almost burst open right there and then. It's the girl with the bubbly hair and smudgy eyes. The one with the guitar at Manchester Piccadilly station, with the voice that's smoother than chocolate.

"You'll have to learn to make the fire," says Beckett, "if you want to keep warm in winter. And we'll have to get you a bike so you can zip down the towpath to school." He pauses then he says, smiling, "One thing I want to know is, how exactly did Blue Bunny find himself in Selfridges?"

"That's a long story too," I say. "And I will tell you one day. But there's more important stuff I need to know. Beckett, what happened with you and Mum?" I ask, "Why won't she talk about you? It's like you never existed."

Beckett runs his hand through his scraggy hair and tips his head to one side.

"That's another long story," he says. "The short version is that once we got to Manchester she had this string of crazy boyfriends. When I was fourteen I decided I'd had enough, so I went to live with my best mate and his dad. It was cool. His dad helped me get my exams done and get a job and stuff. Then I heard that Mum'd had Connor and it made me so mad. She wasn't fit to be a mother, she shouldn't put another child through the same nightmare she'd put you and me through. And I went round there and told her so."

He rests his hand on his lap and rubs the soft bit of skin between his fingers.

"She didn't like hearing the truth," he says. "So she said she never wanted to see me again. And then she went on to have Jayda. Sometimes I wonder why she had any of us. She doesn't even seem to like kids, but she keeps on having more. I worry about them. It's why I visit Connor at school. I watch the house sometimes to make sure Jayda's OK."

"It was horrid in there," I say. "She's horrid to them."

Lizzie's ears prick up.

I look at Beckett.

"We can't do anything yet," he says, "but you mustn't worry. Social Services have their eye on them. They're not invisible."

Lizzie drops us off by the canal, handing us my bag and saying goodbye.

"Ready?" he says, leading the way down the towpath to the boat.

And gripping Blue Bunny's ear tightly, I nod.

Chapter 26

Now

I have a little cabin of my own on our boat. It's painted white and has a tiny porthole window with a circle of shiny brass around the edge. When I wake in the mornings the world is full of duck quacks and sunshine and when I go to bed at night I get rocked to sleep by the soothing swish of the water. I never knew this much happiness was possible. When I was out that night by the Cathedral, with the rain glittering down and no shoes on my feet, I never knew that all this love was swimming towards me.

"Hey," says a man, knocking his fist on the top of the

boat and jumping aboard. "Anyone home?"

"Hey, Joe, come on in," says Beckett, leaping up to greet him. "Come and meet Gabriella."

And there he is. The lemon juggling man with the beautiful swoosh of black tattooed angel wings down his back. And everything inside me crackles and thrums.

"Hi, I'm Joe," he says, making a little wave. "I'm Beckett's mate. Pleased to meet you, Gabriella. How's boat life treating you?"

This big blush rises in my cheeks, knowing those silky wings are hiding under his jumper. I can hardly look at him.

"Hi," I say. Then I think my face might explode if I sit there any longer so I tell Beckett I'm going for a walk.

I walk to Connor's school and watch him through the fence trying to kick the ball in a straight line. I sprinkle some magic dust in my palm and blow it through the air to him. I blow some more to Jayda and go past my new school, which I start at on Monday. I peer through the gate at all the children in navy blue jumpers, looking to see if there'll be someone as special as Grace there.

I go to Manchester Piccadilly station and stand next to Leila. I watch the coins twinkle and clink in her hat and I swim in her chocolate-smooth voice. I run to the coffee shop and bring her a creamy latte and she winks at me while she's singing.

I walk through the maze of streets, past the shops, past the silver people and the man playing the big xylophone thing, swinging the sticks so fast that they blur. And when I get to Piccadilly Gardens, Henny's there, plaiting a girl's red hair.

"Hey," she says, smiling. "You back?"

I shake my head and nod at the same time. "Kind of," I say, "but not really. I found him, Henny. I found Beckett. I get to live with him now on a boat on the canal. Come and see it. Come and meet him. Come and see me."

Henny shrugs. She blinks and wipes her eye. "Cool," she says. "That's really cool, kitten."

She finishes tying the girl's plait and they both look up at me.

"This is Chicky," Henny says. "She's the new girl.

You know me. Cluck! Cluck!"

I slip two of my bracelets off and give them one each, then wander over to Tia. She's sitting on the grass with her arms wrapped round her legs, twisting her jumper sleeve. I sit down next to her and her eyes shine when she sees me. We don't talk about *that* night. I know that she can't.

Instead, I tell her about Beckett and our boat. I tell her if it's raining she can come to the canal and find *Providence*. I tell her if she comes for a sleepover we might have to squeeze in tight like sardines, but Tia doesn't mind about things like that and neither do I. I give her a bracelet and we lie back on the grass together and look up at the sky, making pictures in the clouds.

And then I go into the Cathedral alone. That deep quiet hush drapes over me like the softest duvet ever. And I drink it all in.

All of it.

All the whispering people and the glass windows whose colours fall on my hands, the nave, shining like a golden chocolate wrapper.

I sit on one of the chairs and listen to the choir

practising songs that soar up to heaven like doves. And without anyone noticing, I open my mouth and make a sound that flies right up with theirs, up to the rafters, through the roof and out into the wide open sky.

I find some coins in my pocket and with a steady hand I light one of the little candles on the stand. I watch as it flickers for a moment and then rises bravely up, shining so brightly for everyone to see.

Acknowledgements:

Thank you Daniel for your presence, for your tender heart, for holding my hand as we walk the streets of this wonderful life together.

Thank you my beautiful children, Jane, Tim, Sam, Joe and Ben, for bringing so much love and joy to my life. I am so proud of you all.

Thank you Tim and Susie for your love, for witnessing my entire life, for always seeing me.

Thank you Paul for your constant encouragement and support – for the love that we share – for our children.

Thank you Michael and Jules for cosy bed space when I'm in London and for all your love and support – and Dao, Amida, Nikki and Benita for being my family in Devon, Sura-land.

Thank you Andy McCullough for sharing your own story, for helping me sense what life for a child living on the street is really like and for all your wonderful support.

A big thank you to Rob, Kate and everyone else at Railway Children, and to John, Stephen, Moira, Claire and everyone else at The Big Issue Foundation for being so wonderfully enthusiastic and helpful – and for coming up with so many great ideas.

Thank you Eve for your enduring commitment to my work, for your love, for our heart sharing.

Thank you Lizzie and Rachel for your patience, care and editorial expertise. I feel so blessed to have your support.

Thank you Eliz for the gorgeous cover design, I love it!

Thank you everyone else from HarperCollins who's involved in some way or other with my books. I have so much appreciation for all the hard work that you do.

Thank you Mike and Pete – I'm blown away and touched beyond measure by the incredible gifts you're laying at my feet.

Thank you Sophie for being the first reader of *Invisible Girl* and offering your helpful comments.

I have such gratitude for all the people I never get to meet – those who plant and cut the sustainable forests, make the paper, print the pages, wrap and pack and drive and stack and sell my books – without you *Invisible Girl* would be left drifting in my imagination – Thank you for the part that you play in bringing my books into being.

Thank you Adam for seeing me when I couldn't see myself.

Thank you to the space in which we all appear – in and as this…

Love Love Love x

Afterword by John Bird - Founder and Editor in Chief at The Big Issue

Can we stop children from running away? Can we reduce the vulnerability of the child when they are out there on their own? Places of safety near home, crash pads, and support need creating. Workers who can envisage what a child is going through need to prevent the poor home life leading to the streets. Charities like 'Railway Children' need our support and our attention. For once you get to the streets, the sharks and the piranhas are there for you to fall into the hands of.

The streets the homeless walk, I walked many decades ago. I slept down the back of cinemas and hotels, in little gardens and up alleys. There was always a threat. There was always someone to prey off boys like me, who had only just made it into their teens. But it was a rare enough thing then for a boy like me to rear up against the violence of home life and seek the streets as a better option, rather than stay in a badly behaving family.

Now, in the new century, I would dread to face street life. The threats are even greater. There are no longer the patrolling policemen who roamed in search of the rough sleeper. We now live in a more dislocated society and it is reflected in the amounts of children that reach our streets and seek solace in the most dangerous of places.

We have to tell stories and we have to read stories. We have to read books like *Invisible Girl* and be inspired to do something about children running away. We have to ensure that there is support for children who have abandoned hope and gone off to inhabit the threatening world of street life. I hope that this work will help us understand that we need to shake up a society that can produce so many runaways. That fails children who should have a safety net that works.

Once, a policeman brought a girl of sixteen to the Big Issue offices. She was desperate, having some problems with her exams and her family's expectations. She came from what by the look of her was a good home. But even that did not stop her from feeling that she could not face home life and school life any more, or from choosing a desperate act.

The suffering of children needs not to lead to street life. But if it does, we need the supporting net to pick them up and carry them to places of safety. Away from the ever watchful eyes of those who would exploit them. Many *Big Issue* vendors began their journey to the streets by running away as a youngster. We want to play our part in helping young people think differently about what it can mean to become homeless; our schools education packs aim to do just that.

The streets are worse than anything I encountered in my childhood. And for that reason alone I want to support books like *Invisible Girl*. And support the work of people who try to provide an answer to children's vulnerability. Please encourage others to read this book generously. Tell everyone, spread the word.

Visit www.bigissue.org.uk and www.bigissue.com

The Big Issue is a registered charity by the Charity Commission in England & Wales (no. 1049077).

THE BIG ISSUE FOUNDATION
Charity No. 1049077

Turn over for more great reads by
Kate Maryon x

Maya wishes she could go surfing and hang out on the beach, but as an only child her parents are pretty overprotective.
Cat has the freedom to do what she likes – her mum barely looks after herself…

But now Maya's family are adopting Cat and suddenly their lives collide. As tensions rise and secrets surface, can Maya and Cat ever be friends, let alone sisters?

*"We talk about everything. Dad and me. About all
the mysteries inside of us. About all our wonderings
of the world. But tomorrow my dad goes to war.
Then what will I do?"*

Jemima's dad is in the Army and he's off to
Afghanistan for six whole months. Her mum's about
to have another baby and Gran's head is filled with
her own wartime memories. So while Mima is
sending Dad millions of guardian angels to keep
him safe, who is looking out for her?

A Million Angels
Kate Maryon

*"It was just school to me. I'd been there since I was
seven years old. But I'm not there any more, I'm here
and I need to get on and get used to it, just like all
the other changes in my life."*

Liberty is sure there's more to life than getting
good exam results and earning lots of money, but
her super-rich, workaholic dad doesn't agree.
And when Dad's business goes bust and
there's no money left,
Liberty's whole world is turned upside down...

*"The page is staring at me waiting for words, but I don't
even know where to start. I'd quite like
to begin the letter with something like,
Dear Mum, Thanks for ruining my life,
but I don't think that's the kind of letter that
Auntie Cass has in mind."*

Tiff's sparkling world comes crashing down when
her mum commits a crime. Packed off to live with
family in the dullest place on the planet – and without
Mum around – everything seems to
lose its shine . . .

Shine
Kate Maryon